❧ Mane matted with mud, coat still hanging with sweat, the horse was still an amazing animal. Sam was sure his shoulder was higher than her head. He had to be seventeen hands high. He might be taller.

"Some ceiling padding in that trailer might be a good idea," Dad said to the two men handling the massive gelding.

Sam was confused by Dad's comment until she saw a bright trickle of blood dripping from the horse.

"Shoot, whoever buys him's not gonna mind. He's gonna be flyin' with the angels real soon, anyway," the taller man guffawed.

A chill of disbelief spread from the nape of Sam's neck, downward. Goose bumps coated her arms. They were talking about selling the horse to someone who would kill him for pet food. ❧

Read all the books in the PHANTOM STALLION *series:*

Phantom Stallion

⚘ 9 ⚘
Gift Horse

TERRI FARLEY

AVON BOOKS

An Imprint of HarperCollins*Publishers*

Gift Horse
Copyright © 2003 by Terri Sprenger-Farley
All rights reserved. No part of this book may be used or
reproduced in any manner whatsoever without written
permission except in the case of brief quotations
embodied in critical articles or reviews.
Printed in the United States of America.
For information address HarperCollins Children's
Books, a division of HarperCollins Publishers,
1350 Avenue of the Americas, New York, NY 10019.

Library of Congress Catalog Card Number:
2003090449
ISBN 0-06-056157-2

First Avon edition, 2003

AVON TRADEMARK REG. U.S. PAT. OFF. AND IN OTHER COUNTRIES,
MARCA REGISTRADA, HECHO EN U.S.A.

Visit us on the World Wide Web!
www.harperchildrens.com

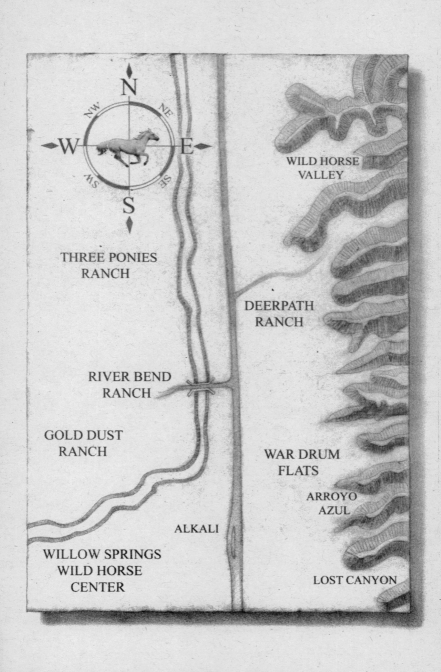

N
NW NE
W   E
SW SE
S

WILD HORSE
VALLEY

THREE PONIES
RANCH

DEERPATH
RANCH

RIVER BEND
RANCH

GOLD DUST
RANCH

WAR DRUM
FLATS

ARROYO
AZUL

ALKALI

WILLOW SPRINGS
WILD HORSE
CENTER

LOST CANYON

Chapter One

$\mathfrak{M}$ustangs danced in the margin of Samantha Forster's notebook paper. She glanced up, afraid Mr. Blair would notice she was drawing instead of reading.

She couldn't help it. Her mind was not on schoolwork today. It was on horses.

Rumor said wild horses had been sold for meat at the Mineral Auction yards. The Bureau of Land Management, a government agency responsible for protecting the West's wild horses, had checked out the stories and found nothing to prove them. Still, the rumors persisted.

One night at dinner, Sam had suggested to Brynna, her new stepmother and manager of the

BLM's Willow Springs Wild Horse Corrals, that the bad guys had spotted the BLM officers when they'd come to the auction.

"I think you should send a spy no one would suspect," Sam had suggested.

But she'd never expected Brynna to send her.

Sam smiled to herself. Her undercover assignment wasn't official, but unofficially, she was going to make sure no mustang at the Mineral Auction was in danger today.

The three o'clock dismissal bell was still ringing when Sam slapped her notebook closed and bolted into the hall. Journalism had been her last class of the day. Now, she was out of here.

"Forster, we need to talk," Mr. Blair bellowed after her.

Sam pretended not to hear, even though her Journalism teacher's booming voice was hard to miss.

He'd only assign her to take pictures of another basketball game or chess club competition. She didn't have time. She was on a rescue mission.

With her schoolbooks braced against her chest like a shield, Sam joined the tide of students escaping Darton High School. She hadn't even taken time to zip her books and notebooks inside her backpack. Dad was waiting.

She'd promised to meet him in the parking lot no later than 3:05.

He said he'd wait until 3:06. After that, she'd have to take the bus home, and he'd check out the auction without her.

The sale started at four o'clock and Mineral Auction yard was forty miles away. Brynna had assigned the two of them to check the horses to see if any were mustangs for sale, illegally. Sam didn't need to check her watch to know they'd barely have time to drive there, let alone study the horses. She took longer steps and slipped sideways between two boys in letterman jackets.

Buffeted by shoulders and backpacks in the crowded hall, she tried not to breathe the smells of wet wool sweaters, pencil lead, and old lunches. Sam figured the custodians swept and scrubbed each weekend, but by Thursday afternoon, their efforts had been erased.

Outside, the February wind waited to slash through her jacket, but Sam didn't care. She'd never been to an auction before and if she didn't hurry, she'd miss her chance.

The mob slowed to funnel out the door at the end of the hall. Almost there.

When another body slipped into the narrow space ahead, Sam yelped a protest. Then she recognized the white-blond braids bouncing against a dazzling purple sweater.

Jen Kenworthy, her best friend, glanced back and winked.

"I'll block for you," she said.

Sam fell in behind as Jen squared her shoulders and pressed toward the door. Wind blasted Sam's face so hard that her cheeks ached. She spotted Dad's truck. It was a good thing, too, because now she had to squint against the wind or risk having her eyeballs frozen.

She and Jen trudged shoulder to shoulder for a few steps. Like all the other kids, they shouted to be heard before the wind snatched their words away.

"Are you sure you want to do this?" Jen hollered.

"Of course!"

Jen shook her head, then peeled one braid off her lips so she could go on, "You're awfully softhearted."

"Yeah," Sam admitted. A squeeze in her chest confirmed Jen's comment, but she tried to sound casual. "Still, it's not like there are butchers standing around with cleavers, ready to make horses into dog food right there at the auction."

"Now there's a pretty picture," Jen said, shuddering.

Halfway across the parking lot they stopped. Jen's bus idled off to the left. Wyatt Forster's pickup was parked across the lot to the right.

Jen pulled on knit gloves while Sam fidgeted.

"My dad said most of the horses just get moved around from ranch to ranch," Sam said, but she heard the falter in her own voice. Dad's assurance didn't make sense. Why would ranchers sell good cow ponies to buy horses whose histories they didn't know?

"You'll have fun," Jen said, nudging Sam's shoulder with her own. "And I've got a feeling you won't come home empty-handed."

"Right," Sam said. "You must be joking," she added, but Jen was sprinting toward the bus.

Jen was a good friend. She was trying to smooth away the worry she'd stirred up. But she couldn't really believe Sam would come home with another horse.

It was an exciting idea, but Jen was a rancher's daughter just like Sam. Both their families believed animals must earn their keep.

Sam smiled as she neared Dad's old blue truck.

One buckskin mare and one half-grown Hereford calf had proven Dad could give in to sentiment. He'd let her keep those two misfits, but she paid by listening to Dad's lectures on how useless Dark Sunshine and Buddy were. It would be a miracle if she left the Mineral Auction with another animal.

Sam propped her books against one hip and fought the wind to hold the truck door open wide enough to climb inside.

"Startin' to blow a little out there?" Dad asked as the door slammed on its own, sealing them inside.

"Uh-huh," Sam said. Warmth from the truck's heater wrapped around her as she zipped her books and notebook into her backpack. She held her cold hands up to the vent and sighed. Then, she sniffed.

What was that delicious aroma?

"Watch your feet," Dad said as he backed from the parking space and headed into the traffic going out of the parking lot.

"I will," she said, then looked down.

A wisp of steam escaped from a little triangle in the lid of a Styrofoam cup.

Sam had never expected the cab of Dad's truck to smell like hazelnut hot chocolate, but it did. Her favorite treat in the world sat wedged between wire cutters and a gray metal toolbox so that it wouldn't tip over.

"Might as well drink it while it's hot," Dad said.

Sam studied Dad as he stared straight ahead. He'd changed in the last few months. He was still darkly tanned and beef-jerky thin, with lines at the corners of his eyes from searching the range for stray cattle in all kinds of weather. He'd always insisted fancy drinks were a waste of money, when you could make the same thing at home for pennies. Should she credit his new marriage to Brynna for his generosity?

"Mmm," Sam said. She leaned back, eyes closed, as the first sip of chocolate warmed her. She didn't care why he'd brought the drink. It was hot, sweet, and delicious. "Thanks, Dad."

"Don't think it means nothin'," he said. His head jerked to check over his shoulder for oncoming traffic as the blue truck labored onto the freeway. "I had time to kill while I waited for you."

Sam smiled. Dad was embarrassed by doing something others might consider fussy. Sam changed the subject.

"Are you thinking of buying any cattle at the auction?"

"Not likely," he said. "Unless you plan to share a seat belt with 'em."

"Oh yeah, no trailer," Sam said.

Of course they had cattle and horse trailers at the ranch, but today they were just spying. Sam flattened her lips, hiding her smile before Dad could spot it. Apparently, he didn't even glance her way, because he kept talking about cows.

"This time of year, I'm thinking the cattle for sale will be old cows or heifers whose calves didn't stick."

Sam nodded. Last February, she'd been in San Francisco, living with Aunt Sue. If she'd been having this conversation with Dad then, he would've had to explain what he was talking about. Now, she knew that heifers—young female cows—would be a lot more valuable if they were carrying spring calves.

"We'll be late for the cattle, anyway," Dad reminded her. "Horses go up for bid around four o'clock."

"I wonder why Brynna didn't come with us?" Sam asked.

"She had to check out a heavy snowfall area," Dad said. "Make sure there was no need for an emergency gather."

Besides managing the wild horse corrals, Brynna made sure horses lived where they were safe and healthy. Using helicopter roundups, BLM gathered wild horses from areas with too little food or water.

"Oh well," Sam said, feeling the weight of responsibility. "We can call her if something doesn't seem right."

After the mustangs were rounded up, they were available for adoption, but those who adopted wild horses didn't actually own them. At least not right away.

BLM checked up on people who adopted mustangs. Only after they'd taken good care of a horse for a year did they receive a document saying they owned it.

"You ask me, she didn't come because she has too soft a heart."

Sam laughed.

Dad glanced her way, shaking his head. "And you are no better. Still, if she thinks there's cause to be extra careful, we can help her out."

They drove a few more miles before Dad added, "Duke Fairchild, who runs the auction, checks to make sure everyone has title to horses they want to sell. He looks for fresh brands, in case someone has forged paperwork on a horse. And if he can't read a brand, Duke's likely to call the brand inspector."

"Like the guy who helped catch the wild horse rustlers."

"Right," Dad agreed. "Brynna says Fairchild watches extra close for stock wearing government freeze brands, and he calls her if he thinks something's fishy."

Dad's tone indicated their trip was a waste of time. She didn't agree, but it wasn't worth arguing over. Instead, she nodded and they settled into cozy silence.

While Dad drove, she watched the miles of winter-tan Nevada desert flow past the passenger-side window.

Mustangs were the most important things in her life—not counting her family. More important than school, though she never said it aloud. More important than her friends, except Jake and Jen.

She loved wild horses' speed and beauty. She loved their silent faith in the safety of the herd. Most of all, she admired their defiance and determination to stay free.

Sam sighed. Maybe she and Dad wouldn't see a single mustang at Mineral Auction yards. Then again, they might have a chance to rescue one.

With a stomach full of hot chocolate, Sam felt drowsy by the time Dad took the freeway exit to Mineral.

They'd just entered the small town and passed its only gas station, when a car horn blared behind them.

As Dad glanced up into the rearview mirror, Sam swiveled to look out the back window. A shiny red truck followed so near Dad's back bumper, Sam could see the faces of the two men inside. With ruddy cheeks and bushy black eyebrows, they looked like twins. The driver hunched over the steering wheel, leaning one palm hard against the horn, honking. His passenger gestured wildly.

"Guess these boys are in a hurry," Dad said.

"I think they have a horse trailer." Sam gasped.

They did. As the red truck barreled closer, Sam saw it towed a rusty gooseneck horse trailer.

"Probably empty," Dad said. He pulled to the side of the road so the red truck could pass. "Planning to buy a steer or some such."

Neither driver nor passenger gave a wave of thanks as they rocketed past.

"They've got a horse," Sam said.

Watching the trailer sway from side to side made her feel a little sick. Through the slats, she could see a giant animal—probably a draft horse.

When Dad pulled back onto the street, Sam could see the horse's huge hooves shuffling, trying to maintain balance.

"Look at that poor horse," Sam urged, as the red truck quickly drew ahead.

"I'm not racing 'em," Dad said, but his tone was disapproving.

Ahead, a sign announced, AUCTION TODAY!

If that's where the truck was headed . . .

But the red truck wasn't slowing. At least not much.

Suddenly, its brake lights flashed, gravel sprayed,

and the truck whipped into a right turn. The trailer bounced, almost hidden by a cloud of dust.

"Ace would never get in a trailer again if we treated him like that," Sam muttered.

"Might be they don't plan on havin' to load him again."

So Dad was thinking the same thing she was. The men were going to sell the big brown horse. Good, she thought. It would probably be better off.

Rows of trucks and trailers filled the parking lot. Dad had to drive for a few minutes before he found a spot to stop.

Sam scanned the pipe corrals, looking for horses. She needed to forget about that huge horse and concentrate on why they were here. They were looking for mustangs.

Dad turned off the truck's ignition, then glanced across the truck cab with a warning look.

"Just you remember, honey, once he's got title to a mustang, a man could give away, trade, or sell it. And he might not be too particular about who was buyin' it or why."

"I know," Sam said.

"Be sure you do," Dad said. He lay his hand on her shoulder and gave it a gentle shake. "'Cause a man might sell a horse at pennies on the pound for pet food."

Sam thought of the Phantom and his son Moon. If they'd been captured and adopted, it could have been their silver-white and indigo-black hides showing from inside the horse trailer. They could have been sold here, legally, for meat. Her stomach turned, but she told herself to knock it off.

Determination was better than pity.

As she and Dad walked toward the auction, Sam made a vow. If any wild horse was in danger here, it could count on her to be stubborn, smart, and more stubborn.

Chapter Two

Sam and Dad were halfway to the auction ring when the noise of hooves striking metal made them search for the commotion.

Sam found the source of all the noise. It was coming from a white trailer freckled with rust.

"It's them again," Sam said.

Dad looked in the direction she pointed. His boots stopped as he watched the shorter of two men pound his palms against the side of the horse trailer. The taller man opened the back of the trailer, then jerked on a rope that wrenched a huge brown head around at a strained and awkward angle.

Dad took a breath, sounding as if he was about to speak, then shook his head. Sam was pretty sure she could read his mind. *None of our business*, he seemed to be thinking, as he kept striding across the parking lot.

"C'mon, you big oaf," said the man yanking the rope.

Sam's feet froze where she stood. The man kept pulling the horse's head around as if ordering him to do a U-turn in the trailer. What was the guy thinking? A horse one-half that size couldn't have done it.

Sam couldn't see the horse very well, but she heard him stamp, then blow through his nostrils. Instantly, she comprehended the message the horse was sending the man. Patiently, the big bay told the man he heard the order. He understood the order, too. Now, he stood and waited for the man to figure out he was asking the impossible.

But neither of the men seemed to understand.

"Back outta there! Back on out!" bellowed the man pounding on the side of the trailer. "Hurry up, we're gonna be late." Then, he switched from pounding flat-handed to using his fist on the side of the trailer.

Still, the big horse just flicked his tail, waiting to be understood.

"Dad." Without taking her eyes from the disturbing scene, Sam appealed to her father. "Do something."

She heard Dad sigh, but she couldn't understand what he was muttering as he strode back. For sure, his sentence included the phrase "puny-minded."

And she was pretty sure he wasn't describing the horse.

"I don't think they know what they're doing," Sam whispered.

Dad's frown said he thought her appraisal of the two men was too kind, but he only nodded, then called, "Can ya use a hand with that horse?"

Flushed and speechless, the man at the end of the rope faltered and looked back at Dad. The other one strutted up, talking.

"Sure, if you've got experience with stubborn, willful mules," he crowed.

"Big mules," the taller one repeated.

They introduced themselves as Mike and Ike Sampson and took turns shaking Dad's hand.

Up close, they looked even more like twins. They both had ill-tempered red faces, black hair, and black eyebrows that slanted toward the bridges of their noses. To Sam, they smelled dirty. Not like sweat, she thought, more like their clothes needed washing.

"Our old man died and we got the ranch, taxes and all," said the short one.

Sam was pretty sure he was the one called Mike, but she wondered what his comment had to do with the draft horse.

"Lotsa taxes," Ike echoed.

Mike did the thinking for this pair, Sam thought. It was kind of creepy that neither sounded particularly sad over their father's death.

"Fella who's running the spread for us now brought in his own stock," Mike said with a short bark of a laugh.

Ike joined in, chuckling. "We sold off all Dad's stock, 'cause he brought his own."

"Told us to get rid of everything with hair," Mike said.

"Everything with hair," Ike put in.

Sam made fists of impatience. Didn't Ike get bored, never having a thought of his own? Just then, he handed the lead rope to Dad.

Dad moved to the left side of the trailer so that the horse wouldn't back over him. Then he bent from the waist, keeping his hand level with the animal's fet-locks. For the first time, Sam noticed the clumps of hair matted above the horse's hooves. She was pretty sure they were typical of draft horses and called "feathers," but the big bay was so dirty, there was nothing feathery about them.

As Dad bent, the big horse relaxed. He knew he wasn't being asked to turn, but to back. When the look-alike men kept chuckling, though, the horse stayed where he was. The men seemed to be watching Dad for a sign of amusement.

Dad wasn't listening to them. He was talking to the horse.

"Okay, pardner, time to come out and see what's goin' on," Dad said. He clucked his tongue and tapped his index finger against the rope, signaling the horse it was okay to back out. "When ya get out here, you'll see lotsa trucks and cars. You'll smell cattle, horses, maybe a few sheep or goats."

The big horse took one step back, then another. He really was huge. Sam thought that if she put both arms out straight, they might be the same width as the big animal. Was he a Percheron? A Clydesdale?

"You're talking to him like he's got a brain," Mike accused. "He can be one nasty bronc, I'll tell you that."

Sam didn't believe it. The horse seemed absolutely gentle.

"He might not understand what I'm sayin'," Dad answered in the same soft voice. "But he knows I mean him no harm."

"Huh!" Ike snorted. "Then you're the only one."

Sam drew a quick breath. Finally the taller man had come up with an original thought, and it was cruel.

"Yeah, ol' Tinkerbell here's gonna be flyin' with the angels real soon." Mike guffawed at his own cleverness.

"Flyin' right up to heaven," Ike said.

For a second, Sam felt dismayed that the big horse was named Tinkerbell. It seemed like a mean joke of a name for such a strong, earthbound animal.

But then Ike's words replayed in her mind. Flyin' right up to heaven. A chill of disbelief spread from the nape of her neck, downward. Goose bumps coated her arms. They were talking about killing the horse.

"Cattle were simple to get rid of. We sold 'em to a fella from Colton, California—" Mike broke off as the horse suddenly backed the rest of the way down the ramp, then shook his shaggy head.

Mane matted with mud, coat stiff with nervous sweat, he was still an amazing animal. His coat was dark brown, but he had short white socks on his forelegs and a light patch on the side of his neck. Sam couldn't help moving closer to get a better look.

My gosh, from where she stood, she was sure his shoulder was higher than her head. Over sixteen hands, for sure, she thought. He had to be seventeen hands high. He might be even taller.

Halter hardware jingled as the horse turned his head. Blinking, he took them all in.

Sam couldn't look away from the horse's eyes. They were twice as big as Ace's, but their expression reminded her of his. Beyond their curiosity, she saw something more. This woolly mammoth of a horse looked kind.

"Imagine feeding such a monster." Mike gestured and the horse flinched away from him. He'd hurt that horse. Sam knew it. Her hands cramped back into fists, but before she could say anything, Dad noticed another problem.

"Some ceiling padding might be a good idea," Dad said. He nodded inside the trailer. She was confused by Dad's comment until she saw a bright trickle of blood dripping from the horse's poll.

"He's too tall for that trailer!" Sam snapped. "You crammed him in there and he didn't fit."

The words burst out before she could stop them. She glanced at Dad. In the shade of his Stetson, she saw him raise an eyebrow. He didn't scold her, or even tell her to apologize, but he did give the men a suggestion.

"Sometimes a bandanna slipped under the halter, up there by his ears, will do the trick," Dad said. "He would've shown off better in the auction ring."

"Shoot." Mike chuckled. "Whoever buys Tinkerbell's not gonna mind a little brain damage."

Ike held his sides with laughter, but Sam involuntarily reached out to the horse. Welcoming the kindness, Tinkerbell extended his nose in her direction. She was a stranger to him, but someone, some time had been gentle with this horse, and he hadn't forgotten.

"Come here, boy." Sam sighed. Before she could pet him, a pink tongue wider than her palm gave her fingers a quick lick. She felt her heart melt.

"Time to go," Dad said.

"But Dad . . . ," Sam began. She crossed her arms, getting stubborn, but he didn't care.

"We'll talk later," he promised, and his tone allowed no argument.

Okay, Sam thought. She'd let Dad delay the conversation, but she wouldn't let him sidestep it altogether. This was too important.

"Thanks for the help," Mike said. Clearly, he hadn't noticed how hopeless Dad thought he was with horses.

Dad raised his hand in a dismissing motion, and kept walking.

"Things weren't gonna get any better," Dad said. "And there's something I need to check."

"What?" Sam insisted.

"I'll let ya know later," Dad said.

Okay, Sam thought again. That made *two* things they'd talk about later. And later would come before they left this auction.

Sam kept pace with Dad, trying to maintain her stubborn determination. It was hard not to worry. Sourness gathered at the back of her throat and helplessness made her hands shake. Saving this horse might be impossible.

Even though the big bay was a healthy, sweet-natured horse, his owners didn't care if he died. No, it was worse than that. They assumed he would die. They were joking about it, treating him like old, scratched furniture that had belonged to their father. They couldn't wait to get rid of him.

Sam looked back over her shoulder. The huge horse was easy to spot. Gentle as a pet, he followed at the end of his lead rope, rambling toward a building marked OFFICE.

Sam swallowed hard. She'd give Dad a few more minutes of silence. While she did, she'd try to figure out what detail about the big bay was tugging at her mind. Her eyes had noticed something that her mind hadn't made sense of yet. What was it?

"Some folks don't deserve what they've got," Dad said, agreeing with her silence.

Sam made a small sound, but she didn't nod. That would only cause tears to overflow her eyelids and go spilling down her cheeks.

Just then a voice boomed over the microphone from the auction ring, announcing a group of six Hereford cows.

"We've got time to go check horses," Dad said. "You take a look while I find Duke Fairchild. The auction manager," he added, in case Sam had forgotten.

Sam felt a surge of pride. Dad trusted her to identify mustangs. Of course he'd double-check if she said she'd spotted one, but she'd come a long way from the days when he left her behind because she'd just be in the way. He didn't have to explain she'd become a useful member of the ranch team. He just treated her as one.

Sam moved to the corral fence.

If these were all the horses up for sale, it would be a short auction.

There were only four. A fat dun pony whuffled his lips across the dirt floor of the pen, while two ranch horses—one sorrel and one rusty-muzzled black— dozed nose-to-tail, as if they expected flies to show up to plague them on this chilly afternoon. The fourth, a flashy honey-maned chestnut mare, seemed completely out of place. She moved like a gaited horse, maybe an American Saddlebred, but her prancing seemed frantic and her eyes rolled white. Although the mare was a beauty, Sam would bet she'd be trouble.

None of the horses resembled mustangs, although that was kind of a generalization, so Sam told herself to look more carefully.

Wild horses came in all shapes and sizes, depending on their territory and the domestic horses who'd joined the herds over the years.

Most of the Phantom's herd had the wide foreheads, delicate muzzles, and high-flung tails of Arabs and the muscled shoulders and hindquarters of running Quarter horses. The herds in southern Nevada tended to be smaller, with light bodies and pale coloring. Sam had read that the wild horses in Oregon's Kieger Mountains looked like their Spanish Barb ancestors, while one herd in northern California showed traits of the cold-blooded draft stock that had dragged tons of redwood trees out of the forests.

She searched these horses for freeze brands, because that was the only way she'd know for sure if they'd been taken off the range by the BLM. Even with thick winter coats, the mark stamped there by the BLM when the horse was captured should show a lighter patch of hair.

That's it! Sam heard her own gasp.

When she'd been studying Tinkerbell, she'd noticed his matted mane, muddy coat, low white socks, and a line of grayish hair on his neck. She'd dismissed it as his natural coloring, but what if it wasn't?

She closed her eyes, concentrating on the memory. The lighter hair had been high on his neck, right where BLM would have marked him.

Sam crossed all eight fingers then linked her thumbs together, hoping with all her might that Tinkerbell was a mustang.

Chapter Three

Sam whirled away from the corral, eager to tell Dad her suspicion, and saw him coming toward her. Beside him, dressed in a Western-styled suit and highly polished boots, was a silver-haired man who looked like he must be Mr. Fairchild. He was leading Tinkerbell.

"You already figured it out," Sam blurted. She approached slowly. Even though she wanted to run and dance around with excitement, she was afraid she'd startle Tinkerbell, so she didn't.

"Yeah," Dad said, but his head inclined to one side. "But his papers are in order."

"In order?"

"Afraid so," confirmed the other man. He took

one hand from the bay's lead rope and extended it to Sam. "I'm Duke Fairchild, foreman of this outfit." His blue eyes twinkled as if he'd made a joke.

"Nice to meet you," Sam said briefly. "But Dad, are you sure? Those two guys didn't have a clue about horses and he"—Sam gestured to Tinkerbell—"is a great horse. Even though everything here is unfamiliar, he isn't nervous. Look at his ears. He's just interested."

Mr. Fairchild nodded. He watched Tinkerbell appreciatively and Sam got a feeling that if the horse hadn't been so dirty, the auction manager would have stroked him with appraising hands.

"You're right," Dad said. "Those two didn't know a horse from a house cat, but they had documents showing the gelding as part of their father's estate. He got title to this horse five years ago from a rancher who adopted him out of the Susanville prison."

"They had a sheaf of records thick as a dictionary," Mr. Fairchild agreed. "They looked plenty genuine."

"Plus, those two didn't seem the sort to be forgers," Dad said.

Sam tried to think of a loophole. Some way to rescue the horse before he went up for sale.

"The prison?" she asked.

"You remember hearin' about it," Dad said. "Or if you don't, Brynna can tell you. There are prisons where convicts work with mustangs, gentle 'em and even train 'em to saddle before they're sold."

Sam nodded. It sounded familiar, but it wasn't going to help her now.

As Mr. Fairchild turned the draft horse into the pen with the other horses, Sam noticed a man who was obviously interested in buying. He had wire-rimmed glasses, a shaved head—a rare choice in this part of Nevada—and he was so tall and skinny, Sam couldn't help staring.

When the gate clanged shut like a cell door, Sam jumped, but the thin man kept squinting at the horses and making notes on a tablet. His hands seemed to work automatically. While his eyes focused on Tinkerbell, his hand slid into his pocket and withdrew a calculator. His index finger pecked at the keys. He stopped, then glanced down. When he looked back up, his smile was brighter than the glint of winter sun on his bald head.

He jotted something down and underlined it. Twice.

Sam's mind raced. She couldn't spend another minute coming up with her own formula for saving Tinkerbell.

"Okay, Dad, here's what we'll do," she began. Dad's head tilted back, and she read reluctance in his stance, but she kept talking. "The bids can't go very high. I'll use my own money to buy him, and I'll get him ready to sell."

Mr. Fairchild coiled Tinkerbell's lead rope into a

neat loop and hung it on a fence post. All the while, he studied her with a half smile.

So far, so good, Sam thought. Dad was shaking his head, but Mr. Fairchild wasn't. And he was in charge of the sale.

"Look at him, Dad," she went on. "He's gentle as a lamb and oblivious to scary noises." As if to prove her point, a nearby group of Herefords bawled and bucked, protesting their loading into an unfamiliar cattle truck by their new owners.

In the horse pen, the chestnut whirled to the far side of the corral. The other horses followed, snorting.

"Probably deaf," Dad grunted.

"Or cow-smart," Mr. Fairchild suggested.

Sam's spirits soared, but Dad looked at the other man as if he were a traitor.

"Look at his conformation, Dad. He looks like a Percheron, doesn't he? What do you think, is he about seventeen hands tall?"

Dad shrugged. Sam noticed he wasn't saying yes to anything.

"He's big, but not fat. He's muscular, and that wide, deep chest . . ." Sam paused at the gelding's low nicker. He looked right at her and she imagined he was thanking her. "All his good points will show as soon as I get him washed and brushed and put him on better food."

When Dad put his hands on his hips, Sam knew

he was still set on discouraging her. "There are at least three things wrong with your idea, Sam," Dad said. "First, you've got no money to buy him. Second, even if you were, somehow, high bidder, you've got no way to haul him home. And third, who'd buy him? What use is there for big horses like that? Folks who farm use machinery, not draft animals."

"I've heard," Sam ventured quietly, "that they're really good for logging. They do less damage to the forest and they can get in places where machinery can't."

Sam realized she'd been holding her breath while Dad made what was, for him, a very long speech. Every second, she expected Mr. Fairchild to nod and say, "Your dad's got a point." But Mr. Fairchild didn't do that. He just turned to Sam, waiting for her response.

"This is what I'd do," she said, wishing for a drink of water to ease her tight throat. "I'd use my college money—" Sam held up a hand to stop Dad's protest. "Only the part from the reward."

"I remember hearing about that," Mr. Fairchild said. His smile crinkled the skin around his blue eyes. "You identified that stallion who'd been stealing mares from local ranchers, right? Good work."

"Thanks," Sam said, watching Dad.

He was looking up a little, as if adding and sub-tracting in his mind. Sam knew there was money to spare. Even though she'd earned the reward at the beginning of the school year, she'd only spent a little on a present for her friend Jake, and a little more on improving River Bend's well pump. What was left should be more than enough to buy Tinkerbell.

"As soon as I sell him, I'll put the money right back in my account," Sam promised. "I bet it will be a lot more than I take out."

"And how are you planning to get him to River Bend?" Dad asked.

For a second, Sam was stumped. They only had Dad's pickup truck and no one would be foolish enough to put Tinkerbell in the bed and actually try to drive. And Mike and Ike had proven Tinkerbell was too tall for a normal horse trailer.

"My horse van might be available," Mr. Fairchild said.

"Duke, what are you thinkin'?" Dad asked.

In spite of his silver-gray hair, Mr. Fairchild looked young as he turned his wide blue eyes on Dad. "I'm just saying I keep it on hand for customers who need it. Obliging customers is good business."

Before she lost her advantage, Sam rushed on.

"As for a buyer, I probably wouldn't talk to a farmer, because I don't know any. But think of using him as a roping horse, Dad. He's even bigger than Tank, and haven't I heard you say Tank is like an anchor when you rope from him?" Sam took a breath. Now that she'd started, a dozen pictures of Tinkerbell in action flashed across her imagination.

"Or he could be used for clearing brush, or someone might be looking for a heavy hunter . . ."

"Or a circus horse," Dad said sarcastically. "But that's all pretty unlikely, hon."

A slapping sound made the three of them look at the man with the shaved head. Sam had forgotten all about him, but he'd closed his notebook and fallen into step with Mr. Fairchild as they headed toward the small arena where the horses would be displayed for auction.

"How about a private bid of three thousand dollars to take the whole lot off your hands?" he asked Mr. Fairchild. "It'll save you time trying to get them down the chute and into the ring. You could be home having dinner before you know it."

Mr. Fairchild shook his head and Sam almost applauded. She was just a kid, but even she could see that the man had no concern for Mr. Fairchild's dinner.

"Don't be greedy, Baldy," Mr. Fairchild said. "I've got to give folks their fair chance to bid on these animals."

The bald man glanced pointedly at the men striding toward the parking lot and the trucks driving away from the auction yards. Dusk was falling and it looked like most people were on their way home.

Why wasn't "Baldy" going home? Sam wondered. And why would he bid on a show horse, a draft horse, a pony, and two old ranch horses? They were all so different. She supposed he might have a riding stable near Reno, where tourists rented horses by the hour. At least, that's what she hoped.

"How about six hundred on the big boy?" Baldy jerked his thumb toward Tinkerbell.

"Sounds mighty appealing," Mr. Fairchild said. "You might try that bid again in the ring."

The bald man was looking smug, as if he'd already won, when Mr. Fairchild introduced him to Sam and her dad.

"This is Baldy Harris," Mr. Fairchild said. "He buys for Dagdown Packing Company."

If Dad had straightened in shock or Baldy had looked self-conscious, Sam might have known immediately what that meant. In fact, it took a few seconds for her to realize Baldy bought horses for a slaughterhouse. And he wanted Tinkerbell.

As a microphone-magnified voice boomed over the auction yards, announcing the horse sale was about to begin, Sam grabbed Dad's hand. She clung to it as they found a seat in the almost empty bleachers. She held tighter still when the fat dun pony trotted into the ring with a rider.

When Baldy plopped himself onto a bench two rows behind them, Sam squeezed Dad's hand as she hadn't done since she was a little kid. But then, she hadn't felt this scared and helpless for a long, long time.

Baldy bid a hundred dollars for the pony.

"One hundred dollars," the auctioneer repeated. "Anyone plan to give Baldy a little competition? One hundred dollars, but say, folks, you do understand how an auction works, don't ya?"

A few men chuckled and Sam realized that if the auctioneer called Baldy by name, he must do a lot of business here. The idea made her sick. She couldn't help remembering what Dad had said about mustangs being sold for a nickel to fifty cents per pound.

"One-ten," a woman's voice called out, and Sam turned to look. She was a middle-aged ranch woman. A mother, Sam would bet, trying to get that pony for her kids. Sam flashed her a supportive smile.

As the woman grinned back, Baldy raised the bid to one hundred twenty-five dollars.

How much did that pony weigh? Sam bit her bottom lip and shook her head. For once, she was glad to be bad in math. She didn't want to think like Baldy.

That lady was taking a long time to counter Baldy's bid. Sam twisted to look at her, but she'd bent to look inside her purse.

Have enough, Sam thought. *Please have enough.*

When the woman sat up, her lips were set in a hard line.

"One hundred thirty-eight dollars and fifty cents," she called.

"Sold!"

Sam finally released Dad's hand to clap as the

woman walked past, smiling, to collect her pony. Sam wished she'd stay and buy the other horses, but at least she'd saved one.

"Okay," Sam muttered, and noticed Dad was flexing his fingers. "Sorry, Dad," she said.

"Don't give it a thought. This isn't a pretty business."

The chestnut mare was up next, and she must have thought she'd entered a show ring. Flawlessly, she moved from a walk to a trot to a fluid canter. The rider's cues were invisible as she reversed, mane blowing like a golden flag. But as the mare passed, her eyes were terrified. She's performing her heart out, Sam thought.

"One hundred."

Sam turned. This time the voice belonged to a rancher who reminded her of Dad. He was a little heavier and he wore a straw hat instead of a felt one, but the bid surprised her. He had to know the mare was no working horse.

Baldy bid five hundred dollars and there was silence, except for the graceful hooves striking the dirt floor as she cantered around once more.

"Going," the auctioneer's voice warned.

"Dad, I can't believe it." Sam gasped. "She's so beautiful."

Sam tried not to cry, but it was such a pity.

At the sound of boots, Sam scanned the stands. The rancher in the straw hat was leaving. "Going . . ."

Over the microphone, a voice rang out again, but this time it didn't belong to the auctioneer.

"Five-fifty," said Mr. Fairchild, crisply.

Without wanting to, Sam turned to look at Baldy. He met her eyes and shrugged. Sam turned back around, wishing she hadn't looked.

Out of respect for Mr. Fairchild, it seemed, no one else made another bid and the auctioneer declared the mare sold.

"He'll get more from her in a private sale," Dad told Sam. "But he can't do it for all of 'em. You know that."

"I know," Sam said. And she did understand, but when the two old ranch horses, the bay and the black, were sold outright to Baldy, Sam still felt sick. Was this their reward for a lifetime of hard work?

And then came Tinkerbell.

The man who'd ridden the chestnut led Tinkerbell into the ring. He had to stretch to keep one hand on the rope clipped under the bay's chin, but the man had a knack with horses. Tinkerbell lifted his knees in a smooth trot. As the man ran to keep up, the big horse looked almost amused.

"Two hundred," Baldy called out.

"Two-fifty," said a young rancher in a plaid shirt. Unlike the others, he stood to make his bid.

"Three hundred," Baldy drawled lazily.

"Four-fifty." The young rancher had moved down the bleachers to stand beside the ring, as if pure want could win the horse for him.

"Five hundred," Baldy bid, then glanced at his notebook and, before the young rancher could make a counteroffer, added, "Oh shoot, make it six."

"Six hundred," said the auctioneer. "Do I hear six-fifty?"

Sam's heart sank as the young rancher leaned forward on the arms he'd crossed on the top rail of the fence. He stared after Tinkerbell, then shook his head.

He was just being sensible, Sam knew. She recognized the look of surrender on his face, because she'd seen it so often. A working rancher didn't always get what he wanted, because the ranch always came first.

"Going . . . "

Even if Dad had allowed her to use her reward money, she couldn't have outbid Baldy. He saw the big horse, who must weigh close to a ton, as pure profit.

Sam covered her eyes with both hands. All she saw was a kind animal with the potential to do something grand.

"Going . . . "

Dad's hand felt warm against Sam's back, but she kept her eyes closed. She wanted to stay in the darkness behind her eyelids. She could hear the thud of the big animal's hooves, but she didn't have to watch his trusting performance.

"Seven hundred," said Mr. Fairchild's crisp voice over the microphone.

Sam looked up. Smiling through her tears, she stared in the direction of the announcer's booth. It was Mr. Fairchild. No one had bid against him for the chestnut. Maybe it was a tradition to let him win. Maybe he'd save Tinkerbell and sell him later to someone who deserved him.

"Eight hundred," shouted Baldy.

No! Sam rocked forward, head down, as if she'd been punched in the stomach. Tinkerbell had been so close to safety.

Boots shifted in the wooden stands. Dad gave a surprised grunt and everyone turned to stare at the man from Dagdown Packing Company.

"Bidding is closed at seven hundred dollars," the auctioneer said stiffly.

"I said eight hundred!" Baldy was standing now and his bare head had flushed red.

"That was our last horse of the day," the auctioneer went on, "and we at Mineral Auctions sure hope you folks will come back and see us next week."

"You wanna go see what Duke has in mind for that critter, I suppose," Dad said. He rose, stretched, and together he and Sam left the bleachers and started toward the holding pen.

She wanted to feel excited, but Baldy's dark presence lurked behind her.

Dad took longer strides than usual, and Sam was

sure it was because he wanted to get her away from Baldy. The man was still shouting in the direction of the auctioneer's box.

"You can't ignore my bid!" he yelled.

But the auctioneer, who'd noticed the ranch woman's quiet bid on the pony, pretended not to hear.

"That's right," the auctioneer continued. "Every Thursday from ten 'til five, we're glad to have you as our guests. Drive safe, now."

As the microphone clicked off, Baldy stormed toward the ring, looking furious. He paused when he came abreast of Sam and her dad. Sam shrank against Dad's side, but just to get out of the man's way.

Baldy was only a sore loser. There was nothing scary about that.

"I know what this is about," Baldy said in a threatening tone.

Dad stepped forward, making a wall between Sam and the man.

"Then maybe you'd better tell me," Dad said. His tone would sound lazy to anyone who didn't know him, but Sam could tell Baldy had made a mistake.

Dad was a protective father and Baldy's harsh expression was enough to provoke his anger.

Sam peered around Dad, trying to see Baldy's reaction.

He slapped his notebook against the side of his too-new jeans, and his eyes seemed to evaluate Dad in the same way he'd sized up the horses. Sam hoped the skinny man had figured out that Dad could snap him like a toothpick.

Baldy didn't look like he'd quite made up his mind about arguing, when he heard boots behind him and turned.

Mr. Fairchild straightened his gabardine coat to sit just so on his shoulders as he approached.

"We had a gentlemen's agreement," Baldy snapped.

In the moment of silence, Sam remembered Baldy offering six hundred dollars for "the big boy" before the auction began. But Mr. Fairchild hadn't really said yes, had he?

"Guess that means I'm no gentleman," Mr. Fairchild responded, but Sam could tell he was saying something about Baldy, not himself.

"No, now, I'm not saying that."

"Then what are you saying?"

Baldy took a deep breath and shook his head. "Guess I'm saying I'll see you next week, Duke. Same time, same place." He started toward the parking lot, then stopped. "But I wanted that horse."

"If he's back here in a month, we'll talk," Mr. Fairchild said.

Sam felt another chill, which had nothing to do with the disappearance of the sun. The big horse wasn't safe yet. A paralyzing cold gripped the back of her neck.

"Fair enough," Baldy answered, nodding.

This time when he stamped toward the parking lot, he kept going.

Sam didn't watch him for long, because Mr. Fairchild turned toward her, rocked back a couple inches, and crossed his arms.

"As for you, young lady," he said, "I was mighty impressed with your little speech before the sales began. You weren't able to negotiate much with your father, but I'm wondering if we can work something out."

Sam could tell his words were partly aimed at Dad.

Dad took a deep breath, then released it in a sigh. When he didn't interrupt, Mr. Fairchild went on. "I'd be willing to go in partners with you on preparing that big bay brute for sale to someone who might make something of him. Would you be willing to do that?"

"Sure," Sam said, but her head spun. How could this be happening?

"First, I'll need a little earnest money." Mr. Fairchild rubbed his hands together. "You know what that is, don't you?"

"No sir," Sam admitted, "I don't."

"It means you give me enough cash, up front, so that I know you're serious, and that you'll keep your word."

To do what? Sam wondered, but she didn't ask. If she gave Mr. Fairchild more time to think, and

Dad time to recover from his surprise, things might change.

"So reach down deep in that pocket of yours, young lady," Mr. Fairchild said. "And hope you come up with something."

Chapter Four

The auction yard lights came on suddenly, and Sam felt as if she were standing under a spotlight as she wiggled her fingers into her front right pocket. She knew exactly how much money was in her pocket. She hoped it would be enough.

All week she'd been thinking of hazelnut hot chocolate, because she and Dad had been planning this drive and he'd promised to stop for the fancy drink if she paid for it. She'd brought a little extra money, too, because it was February and she'd hoped the coffee store would have the little Valentine conversation hearts Gram loved so much.

Sam slipped the five-dollar bill and two ones out of her pocket and held them for a few seconds. She still had weeks to buy the Valentine candy for Gram.

Sam extended the money toward Mr. Fairchild.

"I don't know if this shows how earnest I am," Sam said. "But it's all I've got."

Mr. Fairchild took the wrinkled bills and smoothed them out.

"What do you think of this plan?" he asked. "In four weeks you will have sold the horse so we can split the profit, or he comes back here and we'll see what we can get for him in his improved condition." Mr. Fairchild turned to Dad. "Is four weeks fair, Wyatt, with school and her other chores?"

"Four weeks is about right," Dad said, slowly. "Spring's a busy time for us, and her mare will be near to foaling time."

Her mare. Sam had never heard Dad refer to Dark Sunshine that way. She felt her smile grow, even though they were discussing something serious.

"Is Samantha responsible enough to come through on what she promised?" Mr. Fairchild asked.

It could have been a condescending question, but it didn't sound that way.

Dad studied her almost as if she were a stranger. "If Sam says she'll do it, she will," he said finally, and Sam stood a little taller.

"Well then, partner," Mr. Fairchild said, shaking her hand. "It's a deal. Come on over to the office so I can write you a check for feed and such."

All of a sudden, she remembered Mike and Ike,

the men who'd been so rough and uncaring to Tinkerbell.

"But what about the men who brought him here?" Sam asked.

"Mike and Ike?" Mr. Fairchild met Dad's eyes. Sam saw them exchange a look of contempt. "Shoot, they were in too much of a hurry to stick around and see what their gelding would bring. I bought the horse outright. Paid those boys a flat fee of eight hundred dollars and they were happy as fleas in a doghouse."

It would be easy to sell the draft horse for more than eight hundred dollars, wouldn't it?

"Baldy would give me fifty cents a pound for him. About a thousand dollars. So anything over that's pure profit, and we'll split it."

Could she sell him for that much? Dad's Banjo had sold for four times that, but he'd been a prize-winning cutting horse. Sam gnawed at her lower lip. She could do it, if she could figure out what Tinkerbell's talents were.

As they followed Mr. Fairchild to his office, Sam noticed Dad wasn't saying much. That wasn't unusual, but this didn't feel like a comfortable silence. The ride home could be a lot more pleasant if she had a buyer in mind.

Jake liked his horses fast and quick-tempered, like his black mare Witch, so Tinkerbell was definitely not for him.

Jen rode a flighty mare named Silk Stockings, and even if she'd wanted Tinkerbell, her family probably couldn't afford him. They'd just discovered Golden Rose, their long-lost palomino mare. Though they'd been delighted to find her, the mare was an additional expense. So, they wouldn't want another mouth to feed. Especially—Sam looked back at the draft horse's huge silhouette—one that would eat so much.

The Slocum family had the money, Sam admitted to herself. Linc Slocum was the richest man in this part of Nevada and his Gold Dust Ranch was stocked with livestock from Brahma bulls to pure-bred Shetland ponies. A draft horse would fit in just fine. He might try riding Tinkerbell himself. But when she thought of the sharp-rowelled spurs he wore, Sam shook her head.

It was a sure thing his daughter Rachel wouldn't be interested. After all, the bay wasn't stylish. Rachel cared more for fashion and nail polish than she did for any creature, especially horses, which she considered dirty and indistinguishable.

But Rachel's twin, Ryan, was another story.

Yeah, Sam thought. *Ryan!* He had lots of money and he loved horses. When she'd seen Ryan riding Sky Ranger just last week, she'd been impressed by his skill.

According to his father, Ryan had ridden jumpers in England. Some riders competed in heavy hunter classes, just as she'd told Dad. But it wasn't likely

Tinkerbell could launch his massive body over a mud puddle, let alone a jump.

Still, he was as gentle as a big dog. He might learn to do almost anything.

Sam gazed at the horse once more. Under the lights, he stood alone in the corral. He surveyed things with great interest while a wisp of hay dangled from the corner of his mouth.

Inside Mr. Fairchild's office, Dad called Gram to let her know they were just leaving Mineral and would be late for dinner. Meanwhile, Mr. Fairchild wrote out a check for Tinkerbell's expenses.

Sam felt the weight of her new responsibility as she tucked the check into her front right pocket.

"I'll have a driver bring the horse out tomorrow. He's comfy where he is for tonight, and there's no use disturbing everyone at your place.

"What time do you get off school?" Mr. Fairchild asked Sam as they all walked to the truck. "About three?"

"That's right," Sam said. She couldn't believe how nice Mr. Fairchild was being. She wished she could find the words to tell him so, but she barely knew him.

That made his trust even more satisfying.

Just before she climbed into Dad's truck, Sam looked back toward the corral. It was too dark to see him, but the big horse must have been watching her. When he uttered a long rasping neigh, Sam wanted to go hug him.

Mr. Fairchild must have felt the same, because his lips wore a pained smile.

"Thanks so much, Mr. Fairchild," Sam managed. "I just know he'll turn out great."

"I think so, too. I wouldn't be doing this, otherwise. After all, I am a businessman," he reminded her. As he went on, though, his tone didn't sound very businesslike. "I don't let it get to me, but my place is the end of the trail for so many animals. People, too, sometimes. Ranchers don't sell off stock this way unless they need the money.

"So," he said, running a hand over his silver-gray hair, "once in a while, I like to give a fresh start to a deserving creature like that one."

Dad shuffled his boots in embarrassment until Mr. Fairchild added, "Of course, I'll deny that silly, softhearted talk if you ever mention it again."

Then he and Dad both laughed.

It was the last time Dad looked happy for a while. Nothing Sam said seemed to cheer him.

"I think this will teach me a lot of responsibility, don't you?" she asked.

"If all your chores around the ranch aren't doing that, maybe I'd better give you more," Dad grumped.

"Yeah—I mean, of course they are. Teaching me, that is," Sam sputtered. "You don't need to give me any more."

Sam let another ten miles roll past before she tried

again. "I think it's so mean they named him Tinkerbell."

From the corner of her eye, Sam saw Dad nod. Most cowboys gave horses short, efficient names. Dad was no different. After all, he'd named Ace and Smoke, Kitty and Tank.

"Should I change his name?" she asked. "He could be Coffee or Spice."

Sam thought Mahogany would be a good name for the big horse. Once his coat was clean, it would look like rich, polished wood.

"Or I could pick a name that suits his size, like Goliath or Emperor." Sam looked sidelong at Dad. "And Mr. Fairchild called him a brute. What do you think of calling him Brute?"

"You'd be silly to name him at all. We don't name cattle because we're gonna sell them. No matter what you think, Samantha, that horse isn't staying any longer than it takes you to get rid of him."

Sam's heart beat hard as she waited. Something in Dad's movements as he steered around a low spot in the road told her that he hadn't finished talking.

"If I were you," he said finally, "I'd just call him Horse."

Sam rode along in silence. She felt melancholy, even though she knew Tinkerbell was safe.

Melancholy turned to uneasiness as she pressed her cheek to the cold glass of the truck's window. Her eyes scanned the vast, dark range. Danger seemed to fill every shadow.

How can I think such a thing? Sam wondered.

She loved the high desert, even though most people never gave it a thought. City dwellers, driving past on the freeway on their way west to San Francisco or south to Las Vegas, rarely noticed the rabbits, antelope, mustangs, and vivid wildflowers no bigger than the nail of her little finger.

She loved the desert's colors. By night, its stark beauty was painted in shades of black and charcoal gray. Silver-tipped curves of sand, rock, and sagebrush rolled to the Calico Mountains.

So why had she been thinking of danger? She wasn't a mouse, cowering from a silent-winged owl. There was nothing to fear, when she was safe inside her Dad's truck with the heater blowing warm air and home was just minutes away.

Snowcaps marked the far peaks. Looking at them, Sam shivered, but not because she was cold.

An eerie sensation skittered across her shoulders and down her back. Now she knew what "spine-chilling" really meant. But she didn't believe in premonitions, so what was going on?

Something moved, far out on the playa. Or maybe not. Perhaps a cloud had swept over the face of the moon, changing the light.

A second later, she saw the mustangs.

Night made them all the same color, but Sam recognized them as easily as if they'd been her own herd. Backs frosted with moonlight, bodies dark as tarnished silver, the Phantom's band galloped along the base of the foothills.

"Where could they be going?" Sam murmured. Her excitement waned as she wondered—had they felt the same nameless warning she had?

"Something's got 'em runnin'," Dad said.

He must have been staring after the wild horses as she was, but Sam didn't look away from the mustangs. The last time she'd seen the horses, they'd been in the Phantom's secret valley. If some predator was pursuing the horses, she wanted to know.

"A man used to be able to count on wild things to tell him the first day of spring, but now he needs a calendar," Dad went on. "Used to be, you wouldn't see a single mustang between November and April. This year, I see 'em every time I turn around."

Dad was right. This had been an unsettled winter for the wild ones.

Sam kept staring at the herd, trying to identify individuals among them. Those two leggy ones looked like the blood bay mares she'd seen so often. And there, maybe, was the colt with the pirate patch spot over one eye.

Where is he?

Sam knew she was searching, most of all, for the Phantom. If this was his herd, he'd be with them.

There! Ice-white and sudden, the stallion surged from the rear of the herd. Head high, he rushed through a windstorm of his own making. Torrents of mane and tail streamed straight back as he swerved through the band to take the lead. Ahead of them by a length, his head tossed to the right and his slim legs slanted. Showing the way to safety, the stallion swung away from the road, toward the foothills.

The herd followed. Swift and silent, the horses faded into the night and vanished.

Sam drew a breath. Spellbound, she'd nearly run out of oxygen while watching the mustangs.

If Dad had felt their magic, he hid it well.

"Wouldn't be surprised if those cayuses were what's got the cattle acting up," he groused. "Every year before, I could count on our stock stayin' on the flats near home, but the last couple weeks they've been on the move."

"Didn't you tell me that cattle sometimes headed back to the last place they were happy?"

Dad gave her a look that said she'd misinterpreted what he'd said.

"Sure," he said patiently, "but long as their calves are with them, 'happy' only means enough food and water. With La Charla running strong and the hay drops we've been making, there's no reason for them to leave."

Sam didn't suggest another explanation for the animals' restlessness. Dad was a cattleman. Cows came first because they supported the ranch and every soul on it.

When she didn't pick a useless fight over the

horses' place on the range, Dad nodded. He thought he'd had the last word.

They were nearly home when she realized Dad couldn't feel as negative about Tinkerbell as he was pretending. Once he knew none of the horses up for auction were mustangs being sold illegally, why had he stayed?

Either he saw the big horse's potential, or he just plain liked him.

Sam crossed her arms, feeling pretty self-satisfied. *That's enough*, she told herself. *Knock it off.*

There was no logical reason to nag Dad into showing his true feelings. But she wasn't feeling logical.

"Wait a minute, Dad," she said.

"I'm not goin' anywhere."

"About Tinkerbell . . ." Sam felt her thoughts line up like ducklings. "What I'm about to do with him isn't any different from what you and Jake do."

"Samantha, it's completely different. It's the difference between a gamble and a sure thing."

"Not really," Sam said. "You board people's horses while you and Jake polish them and make them better riding horses. Then you get paid, if people think their horses have improved. The only difference is that I don't know who'll end up paying me. It's no gamble, because Tinkerbell is a good investment of my time and Mr. Fairchild's money."

"Think so, do ya?" Dad's tone was sarcastic, but she couldn't tell if he was amused or annoyed.

"I do," Sam said. "It shouldn't be too hard to make him worth more than eight hundred dollars."

"What he's worth and what you'll get could be two different things," Dad said. "But take your best shot, honey. That's all anyone can do."

Sam nodded, smiling as she looked across the range. The lights of River Bend Ranch glimmered in the darkness.

"Fried chicken tonight," Dad said. His words sounded like a truce. "Your gram said she'd save us plenty of biscuits and honey, too."

"I can hardly wait," Sam said, and then she sighed.

Home always looked good at the end of a long day, especially when you'd won.

River Bend's lights looked brighter than usual, she realized. Was she imagining it?

Sam's thoughts slowed. Too bright. Yellow beams shone from the barn and bunkhouse, though only the porch lights should have been on.

Dad sucked in a breath.

"Guess we'd better slow down." He downshifted and drove over the bridge at half speed. "And I wouldn't hold your breath about that fried chicken bein' hot by the time we get to it. If I'm not mistaken, every horse on the place is milling around just outside the kitchen."

Chapter Five

$\mathcal{D}$ad was mistaken. Not all the horses were loose in the ranch yard, but none should have been.

Gram and Brynna stood guard between the horses and the bridge.

"It looks like they're ready to wave their arms and spook them back if they try to make a break for it," Sam said.

"Looks like it," Dad agreed.

He slowed the truck to a crawl. The tires clunked across each board on the bridge. As the truck passed under the tall wooden rectangle marking the ranch entrance, its headlights spotlighted the horses. Ace and Sweetheart, Gram's paint mare, stood with legs braced wide apart, but Sam worried most about Ace.

Dark patches of sweat marked his glossy bay coat. His eyes glowed red in the headlights. As he turned toward the familiar sound of Dad's truck, he seemed to peer inside. Sam would bet Ace was looking for her.

Ace was her horse, and she didn't believe a better-mannered, more willing horse existed. Nothing fazed the little gelding, but now he looked more frightened than she'd seen him since a fire had broken out in the old bunkhouse last summer.

Sam leaned against her seat belt until her nose almost touched the windshield. She stared past the horses and focused on home. The white, two-story ranch house was lit so brightly, inside and out, that the green shutters and ruffled curtains showed as well as if it had been daylight.

But there was no orange glow. When she rolled down the truck window, she didn't smell smoke or hear the crackle of flames, either. Fire was unmistakable. This wasn't it, so what was going on?

Popcorn was out, too, and that was really weird. The albino mustang was only green-broke. He belonged in the ten-acre pasture. Instead, he moved in a stiff-legged walk, eyes rolling. The way he kept approaching, then shying from Gram and Brynna, told Sam he was eager to escape.

As Dad eased the truck past, Brynna gave them a worried but welcoming smile. She didn't wave and Sam knew she was trying not to make any move that would startle the horses. In spite of that, all three snorted, wreathing their heads with their own hot breath.

Dad coasted into his usual parking place, then turned the key off. He pulled the emergency brake on slowly, instead of giving it his usual loud yank.

"Look at that," Sam said, as she slipped out of the truck. She nodded toward the ten-acre pasture.

"Saw 'em," Dad said.

In the big pasture—where Popcorn should have been—the other horses crowded against the fence, watching Dad. Tank's white-splotched face and Strawberry's roan one jerked skyward, but their eyes stayed fixed on Dad, acknowledging him as their leader.

"Could the mountain lion be back?" Sam whispered.

"No," Dad said quietly. "Look at Amigo."

Amigo belonged to Dallas, foreman of the River Bend for as long as Sam could remember. His aged sorrel gelding was the horse he'd ridden when she was a kid. Now, Amigo nickered gently, sounding as if he had things under control. Nike and Jeepers-Creepers, younger saddle horses, jostled past Tank and Strawberry until the fence creaked from the pressure of their chests.

"Get back, now," Dad told the horses, and though they stayed close, watching him, they quit pushing.

Sam scanned the pasture again. Where was Dark

Sunshine? The buckskin mare was recovering from abuse at the hands of wild horse rustlers and she was in foal. Sam stared until her vision blurred shadows and trees into one dark mass, but still couldn't spot the mare.

"Dad," Sam whispered urgently as they reached the front of the pasture and started toward Gram and Brynna. "Where's—"

"If you're looking for the mare, she's back in the shadows, near the run-in shed, but not under it."

Sighing, Sam realized Dad was right. Sunny's chamois-colored coat was like candlelight in the far corner. She was safe, but even from here Sam could see she was trembling.

Sam caught her breath as Ace bolted toward her. The gelding came at such a quick trot, Sam hoped he wouldn't bowl her over. She got one hand up before he reached her.

"Hey boy," she said, but Ace moved past her hand and thrust his muzzle against her chest, rocking her back a step. She smoothed her hand down his damp neck. The night air was so cold, she wondered why he wasn't frosted with ice crystals.

Ace shifted his weight toward her hand as she rubbed under his mane.

"What's wrong, Ace?"

In answer, he whisked his nostrils against her neck. He'd never done that before, and she didn't know what it meant. But she stood still. If Ace took comfort in her scent, she'd let him sniff all night.

As she stood there, Sam became aware of Blaze's incessant barking from inside the bunkhouse. If the horses had been spooked by a cougar or some other animal, wouldn't Dallas have set Blaze free?

Blaze, the ranch's watchdog, was protective and territorial. If another creature crossed the boundaries of the place he considered home, Blaze forgot he was only a shaggy black-and-brown Border collie and acted as if he had the size and strength of a lion.

Dallas stood between the barn and the small pasture. He wore only a jean jacket over a white shirt, and must have been freezing.

To the left, she saw River Bend's two cowboys. They stood between the new bunkhouse and the old one, which smelled of fresh-sawed lumber and pine sawdust because it was being rebuilt. Pepper was hatless and Ross had his shirt-sleeves rolled up as if he'd been washing his hands for dinner. Together, they blocked the last avenue of escape for the horses.

So why, with five horse-savvy people standing around, hadn't the loose horses been put back where they belonged? Ace tagged along, practically walking on Sam's heels. She joined Dad as he spoke to Brynna and Gram.

"What's up?" Dad asked, quietly.

"I wish I knew," Brynna said, shivering. Sam noticed Brynna wore only jeans and a long-sleeved tee-shirt.

Gram's pink sweater, prettier than it was warm, hung open over a denim dress. Considering Gram ordered Sam to dress warmly even on summer nights, Sam guessed that Gram and Brynna, just like Pepper and Ross, had bolted out-of-doors in a hurry.

"Seems like they all got crazy at once," Gram said, not taking her eyes from Sweetheart and Popcorn. "You never heard such stamping and neighing."

"We ran to the barn and when we got there, the pigeons in the rafters were swooping and circling," Brynna said. "Just in case something was in the hayloft, we turned Ace and Sweetheart out. When we got back out here, Popcorn was bashing his chest against the fence, so we let him join the others."

Brynna looked at Dad. She didn't ask, but her raised brows seemed to be checking to see if he thought what they'd done was a good idea. It had been risky, Sam thought, since Popcorn had been running wild just two years ago.

"He seems quiet enough, now," Dad said, and it sounded like he approved.

Ace's chin bobbed over Sam's left shoulder as if he agreed. When she turned to rub the white star under his forelock, Sam noticed Blaze had quit barking.

As if the dog's silence signaled that everything had returned to normal, Sweetheart blew through her lips and stared toward her cozy barn.

Sam's chest swelled with eagerness to announce her deal with Mr. Fairchild. Now that she was sure

Ace and the other horses were safe, she had to tell everyone. And Jen would be next. How cool was it that she'd have another horse to work with? Tomorrow!

"Guess what—" Sam began.

"That's my good girl," Gram crooned as she reached up to grab Sweetheart's halter. Gram's eyes shifted to Sam, but when the pinto didn't resist, Gram raised a finger, telling Sam she'd heard, but needed to keep Sweetheart moving back toward the barn.

"Grace," Brynna called softly after Gram. "I'm going to open the bunkhouse door so Blaze can check things out."

"Good idea. We'll go slowly," Gram said.

Sam's eagerness to announce her news kept building as Dad rubbed the back of his neck. That gesture meant he wasn't sure what to do. In spite of her impatience, Sam smiled. Dad was so used to being in charge, he was surprised when Brynna and Gram didn't ask his advice.

"No need to let Blaze out and get the horses into a lather all over again," Dad said. "I'll check things out."

Chafing her hands over her sleeves, Brynna kept walking toward the bunkhouse. "I want Blaze to investigate, anyway," she said.

"Are you telling me," Dad asked in a joking voice, "that you trust that dog more than you do your new husband?"

"Of course not, honey," Brynna said as she grinned and stamped her muddy shoes on the bunkhouse porch. "If you want to crawl on your belly through every inch of that barn, you go for it."

Dad shook his head as Blaze exploded through the half-opened door, zoomed past the people and horses, then stopped and raised his nose to sniff the night air. Gradually, his head lowered and his tail swung in an embarrassed wag.

"Nothing, huh?" Dad asked the dog.

Blaze panted, then looked up at Dad. The dog's mouth stretched into a wide, shame-faced grin.

"We'll go take a look around, just for fun." Dad rumpled the dog's ears. "Sam, turn Popcorn back in with his buddies."

Sam looked at the albino mustang, unhaltered and wandering. Did Dad think she could just reach up, grab a handful of mane, and lead him back? It was possible, but . . .

Dad must have noticed her dubious look, because he added, "Just open the pasture gate a foot and see if he starts to go in on his own. I think whatever happened is over."

A low nicker rumbled from Ace's chest and he swished his tail, looking between Sam and Sweetheart.

"Go ahead, boy. You'll be fine," Sam told him. "I need to help Popcorn."

That was all the encouragement Ace needed. He

fell in after his stablemate, lengthening his stride to catch up.

Just as Dad had predicted, Popcorn crowded forward, ready to rejoin his adopted herd. The others didn't seem to notice he'd been gone as they sniffed between patches of ice-glazed snow, looking for grass.

Sam hurried back to the house, but Dad was so determined to discover the source of the disturbance, she didn't think it would be a good time to announce she'd acquired another horse. For a minute, she tried to find Cougar, but her kitten was in hiding. Maybe it was because Blaze was acting so weird. The dog had followed them inside and begun sniffing at the floor, then scratching it.

When Gram put dinner on the table for the second time, Sam couldn't help fidgeting. Of course it would be rude to interrupt the adults' conversation, but it was making her crazy to keep quiet.

Dad obviously didn't understand her need to tell Tinkerbell's story and reveal her good news. Over their reheated dinner, he hardly glanced her way. He just asked Brynna and Gram the same questions, repeatedly, trying to figure out what had frightened the horses.

Sam cut one bite of Swiss steak and stared at it. She just couldn't eat until she'd told the story about awful Mike and Ike, the auction, and creepy Baldy Harris. The gravy on her mashed potatoes was developing a skin. Her biscuit was hard and cold, and still

Dad was encouraging Gram and Brynna to recall anything they might have forgotten the first three times they'd told their tale.

Sam was about to explode with impatience by the time Dad said, "I guess we'll never know for sure."

"Samantha, you must have a theory. I've never known you to be so shy—" Brynna began.

"But you've been squirming like a worm the whole time we've been talking," Gram finished.

"I don't have a theory, but—"

"She's just ready to bust with her announcement," Dad said.

"We're getting a new horse tomorrow!" Sam heard her voice sweep into a high-pitched squeak.

"Is that so?" Gram asked.

"You found a mustang?" Brynna turned toward Dad.

"Yes," Sam said, not giving Dad a chance to put a negative spin on her story. "He's legal. At least, that's how it looks. The owner, who just died, had title to him. His name's Tinkerbell—the horse, not the owner. . . ." Sam drew a deep breath and kept talking. "But the guys who owned him now were trying to sell him for meat."

"It's ugly, but not illegal," Brynna said, grimacing.

"So, how did we end up with the poor little thing?" Gram asked.

Dad gave a short bark of a laugh and Gram tilted her head to one side.

"He's not little," Sam explained. "In fact, he's about seventeen hands and looks like a Percheron, or maybe a Clydesdale, but don't worry, we're not paying his feed bill and he's only going to be here four weeks."

"Or less," Dad reminded Sam.

"That's a mercy," Gram said.

"And to think I sent you to the auction because I'm so sentimental about hard-luck horses," Brynna teased Dad. "Still," she mused, "I assume he's not here for a vacation."

"No way," Sam said. Although she liked watching Brynna get the better of Dad, she couldn't let her new stepmother have too much fun at his expense. "He's a gift, but just until I've polished him up and sold him. Then, I have to share the money with Mr. Fairchild at the auction yards."

"Polish him?" Gram wondered. "What does he do? Pull?"

"I'm not sure," Sam admitted.

"I bet he's broken to harness," Brynna said, trying to help. "A lot of big horses are."

"I'm not sure about that, either."

"But he has been ridden?" Brynna inquired. She said it quietly, as if she was afraid of Sam's answer.

"We'll see tomorrow, I guess," Sam said.

Sam welcomed the telephone's sudden ring, and she was even more relieved when Gram answered, then announced it was Jen. Her friend would understand how exciting it was going to be, working with the big brown horse.

"Oh, I almost forgot." Gram held onto the telephone receiver, even though Sam was reaching for it. Then she talked into it again. "Jennifer, dear," Gram said, "I'm afraid Sam will have to call you back in a little while."

"Gram!" Sam yelped.

She couldn't believe Gram was doing this, but she was. In fact, she'd just hung up the telephone. She glanced at the kitchen clock, tsked her tongue, and then turned to Dad.

"I should have told you earlier, Wyatt, but with all the excitement, it just slipped my mind." Gram crossed her arms at her waist and gave a sigh full of meaning.

But what kind of meaning? Was she sad? Exasperated? Sam couldn't tell, but it didn't sound good.

"Told me what?" Dad asked.

"Mrs. Santos, the Darton High School principal, called at about three-thirty this afternoon. She wanted to talk with you right away. When I told her you might be late, she said it didn't matter." Gram paused and gave Sam a mistrustful look. "She said you were to call, no matter how late you got in."

Chapter Six

$\mathcal{M}$r. Blair couldn't be so mad at her for leaving Journalism when he was calling after her that he'd notify Mrs. Santos, could he?

Dad took the note bearing the principal's number from Gram. He studied it as if looking for a hidden message.

"Do you know what this is about, Samantha?" Dad sounded cautious, but not angry. So far.

"I have no idea," Sam tried to sound lighthearted. "I could call R. J. Because he's editor of the *Dialogue* — our newspaper — he knows just about everything going on at school."

Other than ignoring Mr. Blair when he called after her earlier, Sam couldn't think of a single thing she'd done wrong. Maybe really minor things, like cutting across the grass instead of taking the sidewalk, when she was late. Monday she had been tardy to history class, but Mrs. Ely had been writing the day's assignment on the chalkboard and hadn't noticed.

"Could Mrs. Santos be calling about your grades?" Brynna asked.

"No way. Since Jake's been tutoring me in algebra, I'm getting a C-plus," Sam said. "I told you that."

"Careful of your tone, Samantha," Dad cautioned.

Although she'd heard nothing wrong with her tone, Sam kept her next words level and easy. "All my other classes are B's or better. Besides, most teachers don't involve Mrs. Santos unless . . . " Sam stopped before she'd painted herself into a corner.

"Unless . . . ?" Gram insisted.

"It's something serious," Sam said. "But it might not be *bad* serious. Maybe I won an award or something." Even to Sam, her words sounded weak. "Want me to try R. J. first, so that you don't have to bother Mrs. Santos?"

Lined up like a firing squad, Gram, Dad, and Brynna studied her, waiting for a confession. Three against one. And they were adults, ready to punish her for the slightest little thing.

A twinge of understanding crossed Brynna's face and Sam knew that her new stepmother was the most sympathetic of the three.

"I haven't done anything," Sam insisted.

"Let's end the suspense," Brynna said.

"In just a minute," Dad said. "Samantha, if this turns out to be serious, you're not going to be keeping that draft horse. It'd be too much like a reward."

"But Dad, if he goes back to the auction . . ." Sam closed her eyes. He could be killed.

"It's not open for discussion," Dad said.

"Wyatt?" Brynna nodded at the phone.

Dad dialed. He introduced himself, apologized for the late hour, and then he listened. In the silence, Sam heard the kitchen clock tick.

"If we'd known . . ." Dad shook his head. "How long has *she* known?"

There was no question who "she" was, but Sam wondered just what she was supposed to know. Her nerves cranked tight as Dad continued to listen.

Blaze nosed his full food dish, then walked away from it. Cougar walked into the kitchen and stretched as if he'd just awakened from a nap.

"That's not the way we handle things around —" Dad began. His face flushed. Sam couldn't tell if he was angry or embarrassed. "That's fine." He listened. "I'll see that she does. Early. Yes, ma'am." Dad smiled. "You have a nice evening, now."

"Spill it," Brynna said when Dad paused for a moment. She was kidding, of course, but she didn't look patient.

Dad faced Brynna and Gram in a way that excluded Sam.

"Did you know every student in the school is responsible for doing twenty-four hours of community service? Neither did I," he said when they both shook their heads.

Sam's shoulders sagged in relief. Tinkerbell would be safe. Doing community service wasn't hard. She'd think of something before the end of the year. Everyone did it.

Jen, of course, had started doing her community service in September. She had straight A's in academics and citizenship. Her family didn't have a lot of money, so she'd set her sights on college scholarships as the way to pay for veterinary school. Jen would do nothing to put her goal in jeopardy, so she'd been tutoring talented middle school kids in high school chemistry, for free.

Jake and his brothers weren't angels, but they had created their own anti-graffiti task force. Crammed into their shared truck, they made monthly rounds of the Darton Valley high schools and gave graffiti-marred surfaces fresh coats of paint.

Even Jake's friend Darrell, who had a pretty rough reputation, headed a tire recycling program at a truck stop outside of Darton.

But all of those kids had lived here forever. None of them had been in San Francisco for two years, then come back an outsider. None of them felt the slimy-stomached, clammy-browed terror she did when she had to get up in front of people and speak.

None of them knew for sure that the student council would condemn their projects without listening. All those popular kids had to give their stamp of approval to each proposed project.

Sam hadn't asked for a space on the student council agenda because she knew the outcome would be the same whether it was a stupid idea or one worthy of winning a Nobel Prize. With Rachel Slocum and her mall mate Daisy on the student council, Sam knew she didn't have a chance.

Sam watched helplessly as Dad, Gram, and Brynna faced her. If she told them the truth, they'd tell her not to be silly. She'd ridden in stampedes and floods. She'd faced Linc Slocum and Brahma bulls. Speaking to twelve teenagers, they'd insist, couldn't be scarier than those things. But it could.

"Does Mrs. Santos want me to do a story about it for the newspaper?" Sam asked.

In spite of their disbelieving expressions, Sam told herself it was possible. Her very first story for the Darton *Dialogue* had been an interview with Mrs. Santos, and the principal had been pleased with the published article. Maybe Mrs. Santos wanted help in flushing out ideas for community service projects. For other students.

"No," Dad said, patiently. "She wants to talk with you about your project, tomorrow morning."

"But I don't have a project!"

"That's probably the point, Sam," Brynna said.

"So, what will I talk about?"

"Mrs. Santos has a plan," Dad said.

"Well, isn't that nice," Gram said.

Sam wasn't so sure. Dad was wearing an expression she'd call a smirk.

"What's her plan?" she asked cautiously.

Dad couldn't wait to tell. "Any student without a community service project by spring break will be working at the Darton dump, sorting out recyclable materials."

If it was Mrs. Santos' idea, she might not have to appear before the student council, but the dump always smelled like burning rubber. Every inch of the dump was piled with wrecked cars and twisted lawn furniture, soggy cardboard boxes, and plastic wrappers smeared with old tomato sauce. She shuddered just thinking about it. How was she supposed to sort through that stuff? With her hands?

"Yuck," Sam said. "That's not fair!"

"I think it's incredibly fair," Brynna said. "You've known about this since September, right? And you have to get in twenty-four hours before the end of the term."

Suddenly Sam realized she was holding her auburn hair back from her temples, and pressing harder than was really comfortable. That probably wouldn't help her squeeze out an idea, but maybe her head wouldn't throb from remembering Rachel's mocking voice when she referred to her as "the little cowgirl."

These three adults who claimed to love her couldn't know what they were demanding. Getting up in front of the student council was worse than any punishment—except missing spring break because she was sorting through garbage.

"You'd be making a valuable contribution to the community," Gram said.

"And the planet," Brynna added. "Besides, if you don't like the idea, you still have time to come up with a different one."

Brynna was right, but Sam's head was empty. She concentrated. What did northern Nevada need that she could give? Finally she faced the truth: The place in her brain where ideas lived was echoing and dark.

"What would you do, Brynna?" Sam asked.

As Brynna's lips parted, Dad held up a hand. "Mrs. Santos says this must be completely Sam's idea."

Sam's stomach clenched. Why did Dad want to torture her? Instead of working with the Horse and Rider Protection program during spring break, did he really want her knee-deep in eggshells and plastic bags?

A wave of hopelessness crashed over her. Sam's only hope was that some dream fairy would bring her a solution while she slept.

At seven the next morning, Sam sat in the passenger's seat of Brynna's white BLM truck. The dream fairy hadn't bestowed an idea on her, but at least Dad hadn't insisted on going into the principal's office with her.

Sam was glad. Although Brynna was the one who'd insisted Jake tutor her in math, she didn't take school stuff personally and blow it out of proportion like Dad did.

"Thanks for taking me in so early," Sam said.

"No problem." Brynna glanced at the ten-acre pasture as they rolled toward the bridge. All the horses were where they should be. "I have Willow Springs to myself when I get there early. I walk around, check the horses, talk with whoever was on night watch, and touch base with each of the wranglers as they come in."

"And you like that more than shuffling papers and answering the phones," Sam said. It wasn't a question.

"You bet. I wish the HARP program was a sure thing," Brynna said wistfully.

"Me too." Sam had never thought she'd say those words. At first, she'd resented the Horse and Rider Protection program because she didn't like sharing her ranch or family. "They're funding the remodeling of the bunkhouse. That's a good sign, right?"

Brynna nodded. "It is, but I'm not sure I can pull off the spring and summer programs without a clone."

Brynna loved working with kids and horses. If

the state of Nevada continued to support the program and paid her to direct it, she might quit her job at Willow Springs Wild Horse Corrals.

Sam had mixed feelings about that. It would make Brynna happy, but Brynna's official connection with the mustangs had come in handy more than once. With Brynna in charge, Sam felt the Phantom was safe.

"Wave," Brynna said suddenly. She pointed toward the range, where Dad and the hands were feeding the cattle.

Sam waved, though there was no chance Dad, Pepper, and Ross saw her. She waved because Brynna had said it the way you would to a little kid, and it was funny.

A big truck idled amid the milling red and white cattle. Pepper drove slowly, while Dad stood on the flatbed trailer, pushing off bales so Ross could fill the hayracks in the winter pasture.

Black smoke spiraled from the back of the truck.

"That truck's burning oil," Brynna said. Though they were past it, she looked in the rearview mirror and frowned.

Sam didn't ask for details. Brynna's expression said "burning oil" wasn't good. They couldn't afford a new hay truck and it might cost a lot to fix the old one.

Brynna shook her head and Sam could almost read her mind. There was no way Brynna could quit her BLM position unless the HARP job was dependable. But when Brynna spoke next, she didn't say what Sam had been expecting.

"What are you going to tell Mrs. Santos?" Brynna asked.

Sam shrugged so vigorously that the shoulders of her new black sweater brushed her earlobes. "I'm just going to tell the truth. I have no idea what to do."

"It wouldn't be so bad, working at the dump." Brynna took one hand from the steering wheel and patted Sam's hands, which gripped each other in her lap. Her eyes still watched the road as she added, with a suspicious lilt in her voice, "At least the weather should be nice by then."

The campus of Darton High was quiet. Most students wouldn't arrive until just before the first bell rang.

A flock of chickadees and sparrows took wing as Sam crossed the quad that separated the classrooms from the school office.

"What are you looking for, guys?" she asked as they scolded from the branches of a small tree.

Maybe worms, Sam thought. Though the grass wasn't crusted in old snow and ice like it was at home, everything underfoot looked brown and soggy.

The office doors were locked. Sam saw no secretaries inside when she peered through the windows.

She glanced at the faculty parking lot. It was

empty except for a single black sedan. Betting it belonged to Mrs. Santos, Sam knocked at the office door.

Mrs. Santos must have been listening for her knock. Wearing a long tweed skirt, white blouse, and black tailored jacket, the principal appeared on the other side of the glass. With a cordless phone clamped between her ear and shoulder, she opened the door and motioned Sam inside.

Sam slipped into the warm office and sat quietly while Mrs. Santos talked with someone about a burst pipe in the gym. Mrs. Santos tapped her fingernails on her desk and rolled her dark-brown eyes. Sam figured it would be just her luck if the frustrating conversation put the principal in a bad mood.

Sam heard the bustle of secretaries and students increase in the other parts of the office. By the time Mrs. Santos hung up, Sam had only ten minutes left before the bell rang for her first class.

"Okay, Sam," Mrs. Santos said, finally. "I thought there'd be one more of us."

Mrs. Santos paused at the sound of approaching feet.

Rachel Slocum peeked around the doorjamb of Mrs. Santos' office. Shiny, coffee-colored curls rushed over her shoulder, held by a velvet bow. She wore a flippy powder-blue skirt and a white blouse with a frill at the neck. There was a tiny stitched monogram, too.

Was Rachel here as a representative of the student council? Or had she failed to file a community service plan, too?

Sam glanced at Mrs. Santos for a clue. Mrs. Santos didn't give her one.

If Rachel thought a designer's fantasy of schoolgirl chic would improve Mrs. Santos' opinion of her, though, she was wrong. Mrs. Santos didn't even greet Rachel, just pointed a finger her way, motioned her inside, and kept talking.

"I imagine your fathers refreshed your memories regarding the school's community service policy."

That answered her question. Sam sighed. At least she and Rachel were on equal footing in here. They'd both left their community service hours until the last minute. Without a pinch of dismay, Rachel slid into the chair nearest the principal and swiveled it so that her back was to Sam.

Sam didn't mind. Rachel had just saved her from admitting she didn't know what to do.

"My father and I did discuss it," Rachel said solemnly. "We think a donation of cash might be more useful than a donation of time."

Sam wanted to scream. Did the Slocums really believe they could buy anything? Mrs. Santos couldn't let Rachel get away with this!

Rachel kept her hands primly folded in her lap. Her nails glittered rose-gold. Her tapered fingers looked soft and pampered. More than anything in the world, Sam wanted to see those hands sorting garbage in the Darton dump.

"I wouldn't expect you to suggest anything else," the principal replied as she clipped a silver earring back on the ear she'd pressed to the phone.

"So that means you'll accept?" Rachel stood, smoothing the back of her skirt as if the meeting had concluded.

Mrs. Santos let the silence spin out. She must be considering it.

Then she chuckled. "Of course not."

Sam didn't clap, but boy, did she want to. It was a good thing she didn't gloat, because Mrs. Santos' attention had shifted to her.

"We had a faculty meeting late yesterday afternoon to discuss our plans for students in your situation. I'd been hoping I could talk with you beforehand. I even sent you a note —"

"I never got a note." Sam stopped when Mrs. Santos raised her eyebrows. "Sorry for interrupting, but I really didn't."

"Mr. Blair tried to give it to you after class, but he said you were quite eager to leave school yesterday."

Sam almost moaned aloud. This just got worse and worse.

Yesterday, while she'd been doing a good deed, trying to save poor Tinkerbell, her teachers had decided she was a slacker. It just wasn't fair!

Sam closed her eyes as Rachel explained she had

received the note, but she'd had an appointment after school yesterday that simply couldn't be rescheduled.

"This is awful." Sam moaned. "I don't want my teachers to think that way about me."

Rachel gave her a horrified look, as if confessing that your teachers' opinions mattered should be humiliating.

Sam didn't care what Rachel thought. .

"Actually, they don't think badly of either of you," Mrs. Santos said. "They think you're both leaders. You, with the underclassmen," Mrs. Santos said, nodding at Sam. "And you with juniors and seniors."

"They think Samantha . . . ?" Rachel's lip-glossed lips pressed shut, but Sam knew what she'd been about to say.

And she agreed. How could her teachers think she was a leader when she was so afraid of going in front of the student council, she couldn't even think of a plan? Besides, she wasn't in any clubs, didn't participate in any activities except journalism, and when she'd tried out for the freshman basketball team, she hadn't made the last cut.

Mrs. Santos didn't explain. Instead, as the bell rang for class, she handed each girl a list.

"We'd like your help in putting together a major community project that will involve as many students as possible. Those," she said, nodding at the lists, "are students who haven't turned in the forms stating their intentions."

Crossing all of her fingers and hiding them behind

her, Sam stood, then summoned the courage to ask, "Do we still have to bring this project in front of the student council?"

Mrs. Santos must have noticed her quavery voice, because she nodded slowly, looking sympathetic. "You do," she said. "In fact, Rachel will be abstaining from all community service projects votes until you two have come up with something."

Rachel gave Sam a stare that actually seemed hot. It blazed between the two girls, but if the principal noticed, she showed no sign.

"And, of course, if you girls can't come up with something, you know my safety net project. That's all set up and ready to go."

The dump. Looking for one bit of fun she could wring out of this morning, Sam glanced at Rachel to see her reaction. The rich girl looked frozen, except that her bottom lip pushed out in a pout.

Mrs. Santos folded her hands on her desk. She smiled and leaned back in her chair. "Good luck, girls. Now you'd better get to class."

They left the office side by side, neither speaking as they jostled across a campus now crowded with students.

When Rachel noticed Daisy and her other friends approaching, she veered away from Sam.

"Just leave the bloody thing to me," Rachel said, reviving her faint British accent to sound properly put-upon.

Sam could have taken that, but as Rachel was

surrounded by the perfume and popularity of her own little clique, she fluttered one hand in Sam's direction and added, "I'll tell you what to do."

That was too much. And she didn't care what Daisy, Rachel, or any of those girls thought of her.

"Fat chance!" Sam snapped back. Hands on hips, she stood until Rachel turned around, her lips parted in disbelief.

"I beg your pardon?" Rachel accompanied the carefully spaced words with a glare. "What did you say?"

Wishing they hadn't attracted quite so many fascinated onlookers, Sam drew herself up to her full height and took a breath. "I said: Fat *bloody* chance!"

Sam thought she heard a few scattered cheers as she hurried off to class, but she wasn't sure. Mostly, she was wondering what she'd gotten herself into.

Chapter Seven

"So what are you going to do?" Jen Kenworthy turned to Sam as they rode the bus toward home. Behind her glasses, Jen's blue eyes rounded with curiosity and she twisted the end of one white-blond braid around her index finger.

"I'm thinking, but I'm not coming up with anything." Sam leaned back against the bus window.

Jen studied her for a full minute. When she talked next, Sam wondered if her friend could read her mind.

"I know you've never been into the whole rah-rah student council thing, but now you'd better get into it."

"Those girls hate us," Sam protested in a whisper.

"They don't hate you, or me," Jen said. "That

would mean that they know we exist. They have much more important things on their minds."

"Like shoes," Sam said, returning Jen's sarcastic smile. "And mascara."

"Exactly," Jen said. "But I'll tell you, if Mrs. Santos wants a dynamite idea for a community service project, you'd better come up with something. If she says you'll be sorting garbage, you will."

Sam had a feeling Jen was right. "Since I've pretty much alienated Rachel, I guess I'm on my own."

"I bet if you think of something good, she'll go along with you."

But would she stand up and present the idea to the student council?

Sam sucked in a breath. She shifted her eyes away from Jen's face to look out the window. It was a pinto landscape this time of year. Snow shone white in every shadow. She wished something exciting would happen, right this minute, so she didn't have to confess she was a chicken.

She was terrified to speak to the student council, but while she waited, things only got worse.

Today in Journalism, while she typed a story, she'd also watched Rachel and her best friend Daisy. They'd called other students over to the desks they'd arranged in a corner of the room. Though they pretended to ask whether each student had sold an ad for the current edition of the Darton *Dialogue*, Sam had noticed a lot of stares directed her way. What if

Rachel was putting the word out that nothing Sam suggested would be acceptable to the student council?

"Why are you so worried?" Jen asked. "Your eyes are darting all over the place and your hands are actually shaking."

"No they're not." Sam tucked her hands under her thighs.

"Okay," Jen said, reasonably. "Tell me when you're ready."

Even Jen's unquestioning friendship didn't help. Sam felt boneless with fear. She didn't look around at the other kids on the bus. She tried to act normal.

Sam wanted Jen's help. She just wasn't sure how to ask for it.

She couldn't tell Jen what Rachel had said, because she hadn't actually heard her say anything. She couldn't tell Jen what Rachel had done, because so far, she wasn't sure Rachel had done anything more than act superior.

"If I thought of a good community service project, do you think Rachel would present it to the student council?"

Jen gave her a confused look. "Why would you want her to? If it's a good idea, stand up and take credit for it."

Sam's spirits sagged. Jen wouldn't understand at all.

"If you want my honest opinion," Jen added, "I don't think she'll do *anything* if she thinks it will make you happy. From what you said, she's pretty embarrassed."

"But you told me you thought she'd go along with any good idea I had."

"And she will," Jen said with a nod. "If you convince her it's in her best interest, and that she'd look good doing it."

That would be a lot of work, Sam thought. And if she did nothing at all, the satisfaction might be just as great. A wicked vision swam toward the surface of Sam's imagination. She smiled as she pictured Rachel at the dump.

"It would almost be worth it," she said savagely.

"Going to jail for murder?" Jen asked. "I don't think so."

"No. It would be worth spending my entire spring break working in the Darton dump, just to see Rachel have a nervous breakdown because she had to touch something icky."

"Oh, yeah." Jen giggled. "Can I come?"

Cheered by her evil thoughts, Sam sighed. "Whatever happens, I've got to come up with something. If I mess up just a little, Dad won't let me keep Tinkerbell."

Jen bounced on the bus seat and squeezed Sam's shoulders. "Do you even believe this? We both have new horses to play with!"

Sam bounced in return and her dark feelings vanished.

When she thought about Tinkerbell, it was like taking off sunglasses. The whole world looked brighter.

"How's Golden Rose coming along?" Sam asked.

"She's doing great. Mom, Dad, and I are handling her every chance we get. She'll let me pick up her feet, halter her, brush her tail, whatever. In two weeks, Dad's going to try her under saddle."

"That's quick," Sam said. Just two weeks ago, she and Jen had found Golden Rose living in a ghost town. The mare had been missing for years. "I don't know how much training Tinkerbell has had. It'll be fun to find out."

"Do you think he'll be there when you get home?" Jen asked.

"I hope so."

But he wasn't. Sam hurried home from the bus stop. She moved as fast as she could over old snow that had hardened into ice. Planting her feet to keep from slipping, she jogged against the icy wind, only to find a chore — instead of a horse — waiting for her.

Pepper, River Bend's youngest cowboy, stood near the hitching rack outside the house. Sam was still trying to catch her breath to ask if he'd heard anything about the new horse, when he ordered her to help with an outdoor task.

"Dress warm and get on back down here," Pepper said.

"For what?" Sam asked.

If Pepper's headgear was any indication of what he wanted her to do, it involved a trek to the North Pole. Beneath his Stetson, Pepper wore a wool hat with earflaps hanging down.

"I'd rather freeze than look like some hound dog," she told him.

"You may get the chance," Pepper said. "Your dad wants you to help me out at the stock tanks."

"No, I've got to wait for Tinkerbell."

Pepper grimaced at the name. "He figured you might say that. You can wait out there, is what Wyatt said."

"Out there" meant the snowy, windswept range.

"I don't know," Sam said, trying to sound helpless. "What kind of help could you need from me?"

"Listen," Pepper lowered his voice and glanced toward the bunkhouse. "Dallas's arthritis is acting up something awful. Your dad doesn't want him doing this chore with me and it'll go lots faster with two of us."

"Of course I'll help," Sam said, ashamed she'd tried to shirk a chore that might actually hurt Dallas. "But there's water in the tanks, and the cattle come drink from them. Isn't that pretty simple?"

Pepper chuckled and rubbed his gloved hands together as if anticipating big fun. "While you're in there, make sure you grab some gloves."

There was no point arguing, so Sam hurried. If she dawdled, Dad might make her leave after

Tinkerbell had arrived.

Sam zipped through the kitchen door. Her cold cheeks burned from the warmth inside. The aroma of fresh-baked cookies and the sound of the clothes dryer tumbling would have made a great welcome home, if she hadn't been in such a rush.

"How did it go, dear?" Gram asked.

"Okay, I guess," Sam said, scooping up the chocolate chip cookies Gram had arranged on a plate for her after-school snack. She kept talking as Gram followed her up the stairs.

"Tonight after supper, we can brainstorm some ideas with Brynna," Gram said. "Mrs. Santos didn't forbid you to do that, did she?" Gram asked as Sam wiggled into her long underwear.

"No," Sam said, voice muffled by each layer she pulled on. "While I'm gone you'll watch for Tinkerbell, right?" Sam said as her head popped free of her turtleneck.

"From your description, I don't think I could miss him," Gram joked.

Heater blasting, Pepper drove the hay truck off the main road, then bounced over frozen ruts toward the winter range. It wasn't that far south, but there was a drop in altitude. At least that's what Pepper told her, but to Sam the gray-brown hills and snow-clumped sagebrush looked the same as the range closest to the ranch.

Once they stopped, Sam discovered why Pepper had tossed an axe in the truck bed. They were going to break the ice off the stock tanks.

"This is one reason the cattle are wandering off," Pepper said. He peered at what was probably a frozen surface, while Sam stood shivering by the truck. "Stay back, now."

"Don't worry, I will."

Pepper shrugged his shoulders inside his jacket, then bent his neck side to side, loosening up before he swung the axe. The first time, it struck with a dull thud; the next time, with sort of a glassy clunk.

He kept at it while she gazed across the range. It was bleak and empty. There wasn't a road or car in sight. Still, if Mr. Fairchild's horse van came near, the pale expanse of winter desert might show it, or she might hear its engine.

He'd promised to come today, but she didn't know what the weather was like out in Mineral.

More than once, she'd heard that the desert's basin and range surface led to "microclimates." So, although the sky overhead was blue and clear with just a few snowflakes sprinkling down, there could be a blizzard forty miles away in Mineral.

As if to prove the notion, a gust of wind screamed across the range and struck them full force. Sam staggered a step at its impact. Then she wrapped her arms around herself.

"Pretty soon, it'll be your turn," Pepper said, as he hefted the axe again. "That'll warm you up."

Sam looked at the glittering axe head. In a blurry silver swathe, it crashed down once more. She was strong, but not tall enough to get the right angle to crack the surface of the ice. Pepper stopped, placed the axe back in the truck bed, and shucked off his coat. "Now," he said, using his shirt-sleeve to wipe his perspiring forehead. "I'll move down to the next tank while you clear this one."

Sam stood on tiptoe. Big gray chunks of ice floated like icebergs in the water. Her gloved hands closed in fists. He couldn't mean what she thought he did.

"Clear it?" she asked.

"A deicer would be better, but we don't have one. For now, you and me are it."

For ten minutes, Sam concentrated on picking out the ice chunks and throwing them on the ground. When she looked up, she was surrounded by cattle.

They looked like prehistoric beasts, only redder and curlier. Pink-rimmed and watchful, their eyes looked weak. Their white faces ended in ice beards formed by drool. The poor things were wishing she'd hurry.

"You are thirsty, aren't you?" she asked.

Range-wild, the cattle rolled their eyes and swayed, but they stayed put. Usually, they'd make a run for a place beyond the sound of her voice.

"All done," she said, then followed after Pepper.

She continued throwing the chunks onto the frozen ground until she heard him grunt. When Sam looked up, Pepper stood there, axe dangling from one hand, eyes on the range.

"Freeloaders," he said.

Mustangs clustered in a cleft between two gray hills. They stood only two or three abreast, so it was hard to see all of them, but Sam recognized them from the Phantom's herd, and she was pretty sure he stood in the back, glowing silver.

The wild horses weren't grazing. Heads up, they stared as if they'd been hypnotized. They were hungry and thirsty, too. Only the tantalizing scents of hay and water held them near the humans they feared.

"They're not freeloaders," Sam tried to shout, but her teeth chattered. "I d-did some of the w-work. And I s-say they can drink from our t-t-tanks."

Pepper stared at her. Sam glared back, feeling her father's stubbornness dancing along her nerves. Pepper had better not laugh, because she was serious.

"You're not workin' hard enough if you're still so sassy," Pepper said. Then, before he turned back to his work, he pointed. "That a new one?"

A young bay stallion with a mane that stuck up like a Mohawk haircut shuffled restlessly on the fringes of the Phantom's herd.

"It's Spike," Sam said in surprise. "He was in a bachelor band with Moon and Yellow Tail. He's never been with them before."

"Must be four years old, at least," Pepper said. "I'm surprised Phantom's letting him hang around."

In his woolly winter coat Spike didn't look like much of a threat. He looked awkward and gawky.

Bellies rounded with foals, the mares moved slowly, ears twisting toward the cattle. The adolescent horses stayed close to their mothers, heads bobbing against the mares' lean flanks, tails swishing as if the snowflakes were flies.

"They're just killing time 'til we're out of here, then they'll come down to the hayracks." Pepper sounded disgusted.

"Wouldn't you? There's not much to eat in the mountains and most of the grass has been killed off by the cold."

"Just the same," Pepper said.

Sam knew what he meant.

River Bend Ranch couldn't afford to let the horses devour the hay that had been carefully bred to have thin stems and lots of leafy green nutrition. They'd worked hard to get that hay matured in the heat, harvested, baled, and into the barn before it was ruined by thunderstorms.

"Don't tell Dad you saw them," Sam said.

"'Course I'll tell him," Pepper snapped as if she'd insulted him. "He's my boss. This ranch is my responsibility, too. Got no job if it goes under."

Although the highway was miles away, the sudden racket of tire chains carried to them, just as Sam had hoped.

The herd huddled closer together and the Phantom crowded forward, placing himself between the noise and his family. But he didn't urge them to run.

Sam felt a stab of guilt. The horses should be scared. For their own safety, they should bolt into a terrified gallop. It was partly her fault they didn't, but excitement kept her from brooding.

"That's the van!"

"We're 'bout done, anyway," Pepper said.

Sam slipped once running back to the truck, but she didn't complain when Pepper hauled her to her feet by one arm. She could only think of Tinkerbell.

"You're gonna love him, Pepper. He is the neatest horse!"

"Uh-huh," Pepper said. He revved the truck's engine and they were about to go when he cast one backward look toward the mustangs.

"Hurry," Sam said, and though she felt a little worried, she told herself the mustangs could take care of themselves.

Chapter Eight

"Go fast," Sam urged Pepper.

Pepper frowned and held up his hand as if listening to the hay truck's engine.

"Hmm," he said then, shrugged, and looked to see if she'd continue.

"We've got to beat him across the bridge so that I have time to call Jake."

She hadn't seen Jake at school today. She rarely did once he started track season. During lunch, there were team meetings with the coach. After school, there were long training runs. It was Jake's only school sport and the only time all year his dad not only excused him from a few chores, but let him spend money on expensive running shoes. She knew

Jake was busy, but all at once she felt she had to share Tinkerbell's arrival with him.

Pepper laughed. "You think he'll want to see your rescuee?"

Sam realized she was leaning forward, as if she could make the truck go faster. She sat back and crossed her arms. "I know he will," she said.

She didn't give Jake a choice. Before Pepper had stopped the truck, she leaped out. Glad her father wasn't there to see her flying dismount, she bolted into the house and dialed.

"Jake," she blurted, before he'd finished saying hello. "You've got to come over here."

"What's wrong?" Jake's voice was level, but forceful. Anyone would have felt compelled to answer.

"Nothing's wrong. Something's right."

"Yeah, well . . ."

"Really right, Jake," she insisted. "I've got a new horse."

Sam hung up without listening to another word. She knew Jake Ely well. He'd been her friend so long, she could predict what he'd do next. He'd ask questions and make excuses using so few words, she wouldn't be able to tell what he was really thinking.

He was sixteen, three years older than her, and he pretended to be mature. First, he'd say something like, "Didn't know money grew on trees over at River Bend." Then, he'd complain he never had time to run.

Next, he'd tell her how much work he had to do

and ask if she expected him to rush over on such short notice.

By hanging up, she figured they could skip the first two annoying steps. Maybe, eventually, she'd break him of the habit of lecturing her.

The squeal of brakes and the sound of big doors opening brought Sam running outside. Tinkerbell was here.

The big bay was still inside the horse van. Head cocked to one side, he surveyed River Bend Ranch from the safety of the van. He wanted to study his new home before he came down that ramp.

Mr. Fairchild had apparently decided to deliver the horse himself. He stood behind the open truck, holding the lead rope attached to the big horse's halter.

Moving with the dignity of a knight's charger, Tinkerbell considered the ramp slanting down from the back of the horse van. With one ear turned forward and one back, he sniffed. Then, his heavy black mane shifted forward on his neck and he marched down the carpeted ramp as if he'd done it every day for years.

Mr. Fairchild smiled as Gram, Ross, and Pepper joined Sam's gasp of admiration. He was sort of a showman, Sam realized. He was proud of his role in saving Tinkerbell and glad the horse was a magnet for so many eyes.

But Sam only cared for Tinkerbell.

"Hey, good boy. We met at the auction, okay?" Sam approached slowly, holding her hand out.

Tinkerbell must have recalled her scent or shape. As before, he gave her palm a lick. It tickled and Sam laughed, but quietly.

She didn't rush to take his lead rope from Mr. Fairchild, either. She only had a few weeks to forge the gelding's trust in her. She had to do everything right the first time. Now, that meant giving Tinkerbell time to check out his new home.

"Oh, what a beauty." Gram sighed.

He was mud-caked, in need of a bath and brushing, but Tinkerbell's thick mane and forelock, his muscular shoulders and sheer size, made him magnificent.

Gram sidled up to the horse. "I remember you."

"You do?" Sam kept her voice low, but she was startled by Gram's affectionate claim.

"Almost." Gram let the big horse sniff her hand before stroking his shoulder. "He's just like the horses my grandfather had."

Sam tried to do quick calculations, but the math was too much for her. Gram must have known those horses at least forty years ago.

"They cleared land of brush and pulled out boulders, helping him turn forest into farmland. They plowed before seed was planted and they pulled the wagon that took the harvest to town."

Gram stared into Tinkerbell's eyes, and Sam remembered how she'd done the same thing at the auction yard. There was something hypnotic and human about the gelding's big brown eyes.

"They were stout, sweet horses who'd break their hearts pulling for you," Gram finished, then she gave an embarrassed shrug in Mr. Fairchild's direction and Sam realized she should have introduced him to everyone.

But Mr. Fairchild beat her to the duty.

"Duke Fairchild," he said, holding his hand out to Gram. He wore a navy-blue Western shirt with pearl snaps that glinted the same silver-gray of his hair. "And I agree. He's a fine-looking animal. I couldn't let him go to the dogs."

Sam felt chills as if she were hearing that expression for the first time. Now, she understood what it really meant. If he'd been sold to Baldy Harris from the Dagdown Packing Company, Tinkerbell could have been slaughtered for dog food by now.

"Since I'm the steadiest driver I know—snow chains not withstanding—I decided to bring him myself."

"Did you find out anything else about him?" Sam asked.

"Just that he's a mustang. I was hoping Wyatt's new wife—"

"Brynna," Gram supplied.

"Could read his brand and tell us where he came from. He's got cold blood, obviously. I'd bet there's a Percheron in the family."

"He's not the right color for a Percheron. They're

mostly grays and blacks," Pepper mused. "But my Daddy says there's no bad color for a good horse."

"He's a gentleman of a horse," Mr. Fairchild agreed. "But not perfect. Oh, he's got no runny eyes or nose, no lumps, bumps, or scars other than the freeze brand. But, just for a lark I tried to get a bridle on him, and he won't have it. Backs away politely, of course, but there's no convincing him to lower his head. And when you pull it down and he pulls up, you'd better get out of the way. Then his nose tilts way up as if he was trying to chin himself on the moon."

Sam stifled the urge to shush Mr. Fairchild. A head-shy horse wasn't incurable, but there was rampant paranoia over her safety on this ranch. She didn't want Mr. Fairchild cautioning her in front of Gram and the cowboys. At least Dad wasn't here to listen. He'd remember the time he'd seen her right after the Phantom had accidentally given her a nose-bleed.

Unfortunately, Mr. Fairchild wasn't receiving the *shut up* brain waves she was sending.

"Now part of that reluctance to be bridled," Mr. Fairchild went on, "could be because of the injury those two yahoos inflicted on him—"

"He was bleeding from the poll," Sam explained to the group. "They had him crammed into a trailer that was too small for him."

The others made sounds of disgust.

"But it's possible he hasn't been ridden. Speaking

of that, you'll want to measure him carefully before you do try to put a bridle and saddle on him."

Sam stared at the gelding's head. It was surely as long as her arm, from shoulder to wrist. Maybe longer.

Tinkerbell dipped his head as if her staring embarrassed him, and Sam recalled how Mike or Ike had called him a "big oaf." The poor horse had a right to feel self-conscious.

"We'll take our time, won't we, boy?" Sam asked him. "And we'll figure out what to do." Jake had braided a leather headstall for his Dad's horse. There was no reason she couldn't do the same thing for Tinkerbell. Maybe out of horsehair.

Where was Jake? She felt a dip of disappointment, realizing he hadn't obeyed her orders. Maybe bossing him wasn't the way to get him to move more quickly. Maybe if she hadn't put her plea in the form of an order, he'd be here by now.

Sam glanced toward the bridge and noticed something strange. All ten horses were lined up along the fence in the big pasture. Buddy, her half-grown Hereford orphan, bucked and mooed, jockeying for a position along the rails, but the horses didn't seem to mind if they blocked the calf's view. Not one of them had greeted or warned off the big gelding, but they all watched, fascinated.

Down in the barn corrals, Sweetheart, in her new turquoise and purple blanket, stared with pinto ears tilted his way. But even Ace, never shy about neighing his jealousy, was silent.

Sam recalled how the horses over at the Gold Dust Ranch had reacted to a herd of ponies. They'd been half afraid, uncertain whether the little creatures were equine. Maybe the River Bend horses felt the same way about Tinkerbell.

"Oh, lands," Gram said, gripping the edges of the apron she wore tied over her denim skirt. "My beef stew should've been stirred ages ago. It'll be stuck to the pot for sure." She turned toward the house, then stopped. "Not that it sounds too appetizing put that way, but will you stay for dinner, Mr. Fairchild?" She glanced toward the mountains, telling time by the sun, which had vanished behind them. "Wyatt and Brynna should be along soon."

Mr. Fairchild declined. "Homemade stew sounds like heaven, but no ma'am, I'm afraid I can't stay. I don't trust the look of those clouds."

Ross and Pepper nodded in agreement.

"I'll just drive on out of here," Mr. Fairchild continued, "soon as Samantha's had a chance to lead the horse to his new place."

Dad had given her permission to use Buddy's big box stall in the barn, so Sam started walking. With most horses, she held one hand at the end of the lead rope and the other just below his chin. That was impossible with Tinkerbell. She couldn't reach that high, even on tiptoe. But it didn't seem to matter to

Tinkerbell. He showed no inclination to trot off in the other direction, although he could have done it effortlessly if he'd wanted.

As Sam walked, she felt strange. Not afraid, but humbled. Who was she to be leading this giant of an animal? Why did he listen to her voice and follow her directions?

The gelding's looming presence cast her in shadow. She was alone with him, although she could almost feel the others' eyes upon her.

He only has me to depend on, she realized. *He could live or die depending on my efforts to prove he's worth something.* The weight of responsibility settled over her shoulders like a heavy blanket.

They were almost to the barn when the sound of the departing van clunking over the bridge made the horse turn and stare with longing.

She should have said a more formal thank you, Sam thought. She should have at least said good-bye.

Tinkerbell's nostrils vibrated in a silent farewell to the last person who'd been kind to him. Sam wished she knew the big horse well enough to give him a reassuring hug, but she didn't. For now, words would have to do.

"Hey, big boy, do you know the story of the lion and the mouse?"

The gelding's giant head turned to face her. He lowered his muzzle level with Sam's chin. His ears flicked forward, recognizing a question in her tone.

As much as she liked him, she felt a little intimidated. Still, she held her ground.

"No?" she asked gently. "It goes like this. A big strong lion catches a little teeny mouse. The mouse promises that if the lion sets him free, he'll do him a favor someday." Sam continued walking toward the barn, talking, telling the horse the story so that he'd come to know the sound of her voice as comfort.

"Of course the lion thinks it's a riot, but while he's laughing, he lets the mouse go. Then, one day long after that—and this is where it gets to be like you and me—the lion is captured in a net. He can't get free, no matter how strong he is, and hunters are coming to kill him."

Sam winced a little. The story came a little too close to real life. It was lucky the big horse couldn't understand.

"Suddenly," Sam went on, "the little mouse shows up and starts gnawing for all he's worth on the net. Pretty soon, the fibers break apart and the lion is free." Sam took a breath. "And the moral of the story is . . . Gee, I don't know, boy. Help can come from unlikely places? Or unlikely people, I guess. Even someone half—or a quarter—your size. Hey!"

Sam broke off as Tinkerbell nudged the middle of her back. She stumbled forward. Her eyes widened and she saw the ground coming up quick. Keeping her grip on the rope, she fought to stay upright, and then Tinkerbell stopped.

At once, she was jerked back by the horse's sheer weight. She spread her boots wide for balance. Then, feeling a little dizzy, Sam turned to face him.

Tinkerbell lowered his head until his eyes were level with hers. He nodded, and his muzzle came toward her. His lips nibbled at the front of her sweater and he blew through them. Sweet alfalfa breath gusted all around her.

"Was that a thank you?" Sam asked as the horse kept watching her. And then, he licked her cheek.

Somewhere she'd heard that only the strong could be gentle. In Tinkerbell's case, it was true. And he deserved her help.

Carefully, slowly, hoping he wouldn't jerk his head skyward at her approach, Sam leaned forward and kissed the gelding's nose.

"There's a 'happily ever after' out there waiting for you," she promised Tinkerbell. "And the two of us will find it."

Chapter Nine

$\mathscr{T}$he biggest box stall on River Bend Ranch was waiting for Tinkerbell. Layered with fresh, golden straw, it smelled like summer.

"Hey, Ace," Sam called to her horse, making a smooching noise to lure him to the side of his stall. "This is Tinkerbell. He's a new guy."

Ace sidled up to the gate of his stall, ears pointed toward Tinkerbell. He looked interested, almost friendly, until she noticed his tight mouth and the little frown lines above his eyes.

"Don't be jealous, Ace," she pleaded. "He's had a bad few months. He could use a friend."

Ace slung his head over the side of his stall and stretched in Tinkerbell's direction. Although his mouth stayed closed, Sam didn't think it was a warm welcome. She had the feeling Ace would give the other gelding a bite if he could reach him.

Tinkerbell must have gotten the same impression, because he didn't extend his nose to return the greeting.

At first Sam was irritated. If any horse should be nice, it should be Ace. The reason he had his own stall in the barn was because the horses in the ten-acre pasture picked on him.

Sam sighed. No matter how smart he was, she guessed she couldn't expect Ace to make the connection between getting kicked and being nice.

"Ace isn't usually this cranky," Sam said, making excuses for her horse to Tinkerbell. "But we haven't been out for a couple days."

Tinkerbell wasn't taking any chances. He ignored Ace and Sweetheart and looked up. Tinkerbell's skin shivered and he sidestepped.

Sam looked up, too. The barn rafters creaked as if someone were walking on the barn roof. No one was, of course, but she could see why the horse was a little spooked.

"It's just the wind, boy," Sam told him. "The old part of the barn is kind of drafty."

The barn was over a century old. Boards and nails had been added by each new generation, until it was a big, rambling structure. Dad was always saying the oldest part of the barn, which housed Sweetheart and Ace, needed to be shored up and strengthened.

Dallas claimed things were built to last in the old days, and it would be foolish to mess with the stout timbers supporting the roof.

Sam clucked to Tinkerbell, trying to regain his attention. "Hey, don't worry. You're across the aisle from them, in the newer part. You won't hear the wind howl so much over here." Tinkerbell shook his mane, stamped, and followed Sam into the stall.

"After you sniff around for a minute, I'll cross-tie you, big boy," Sam said. "No offense, but if you got startled, you could stomp me into a pancake."

Sam gave the lead rope some slack and let Tinkerbell investigate his bedding. He took an experimental mouthful and chewed. As he did, he surveyed his new home.

Sam didn't expect trouble from Tinkerbell, but even a small horse like Ace could hurt her accidentally. Besides, Tinkerbell's handling hadn't always been kind and considerate. She wouldn't blame him if he'd developed some bad habits. So she couldn't take any risks. If Tinkerbell injured her, even accidentally, it might endanger her chance to give him a new life.

Once she'd run ropes from his halter to rings in both sides of the stall, Sam picked up her basket of grooming tools. Then she took a step back and gazed up at the horse like a country girl gaping at a skyscraper. This would be a mighty big job. She had about an acre of horsehide to brush. And those hooves! Sam looked down and swallowed hard. They were as big as her head! Maybe she'd wait until Dad was around to tackle those.

Sam started to work with a rubber curry comb, using soothing, circular movements. After a few strokes, she realized Tinkerbell's skin kept twitching as if she were a pesky fly.

"A little harder?" she asked the horse. She bore down more firmly on the wooden brush. When Tinkerbell stretched and sighed, she figured he liked more pressure than Ace did. It worked better, too, taking off months of mud, caked-on dirt, and sweat.

"That feels just like a massage, doesn't it, Tink?" she asked the horse.

It helped that he liked it, otherwise the amount of dirt and hair swirling all around her might have made Sam stop. She coughed, but tried to do it with her lips closed. She squinted, hoping her lashes would keep the particles out of her eyes.

After a good thirty minutes of work, Sam stepped back, blew her bangs out of her eyes, and looked up at the horse. She'd made an improvement, but she wasn't even close to finished. What time was it? Sam glanced toward the barn door and saw darkness had fallen. She wasn't hungry, but it must be dinnertime. She was sort of surprised neither Dad nor Brynna had come out to check on her.

Take it as a compliment, Sam told herself. Clearly,

they didn't think she needed any help.

Just the same, she was a little afraid to work on Tinkerbell's tail. It was a matted mess and getting out the tangles would be nerve-wracking for them both.

Sam thought for a moment. Her goal here wasn't just to make the horse clean. She wanted to calm Tinkerbell and teach him her touch. It might frighten him if she got a step stool to do his back and mane, so those jobs would just have to wait.

Instead, she slipped her hand under the strap of her biggest, softest brush and set to work on the rest of him, all over again.

A few seconds later, Tinkerbell groaned.

Ace and Sweetheart jerked, and their hooves thudded as they moved to the far sides of their stalls. Sam jumped back, too, and held her breath.

She didn't think she'd hurt the horse. The sound didn't have the tone of an equine protest.

The big gelding leaned forward and his head drooped as low as the ropes would allow. Tinkerbell had settled into a doze.

Sam smiled. She was glad the horse was relaxing, and she was excited to have a month to work with him. Even though he weighed about a ton, Tinkerbell was cute.

Sam worked on, humming and wondering what kind of work had built the heavy muscles in Tinkerbell's gaskins. More than that, she wondered exactly how tall he was.

Ace's questioning snort alerted her to the sound of approaching boots. Since Sam had just moved around to groom Tink's wide, deep chest, she didn't look up. It was probably Dad. He'd finally arrived to tell her to come inside and eat—or start her homework, even though it was Friday night.

She'd do it if she had to, but right now she felt more at ease here in the barn. Inside, everyone was certain to grill her about her community service project. Sam refused to think about the project or Rachel or anything except the soft hair covering the gelding's wide chest.

Suddenly, it moved toward her.

"Got a bran mash, here, from your—" Jake gasped in uncharacteristic amazement. "Holy guacamole, he's big enough to shade an elephant!"

"Shh!" Sam hissed. She dodged away from the startled draft horse, thankful she'd cross-tied him.

Tinkerbell pulled on the ropes, trying to turn his head to see what was making all the racket. She moved in close so that he'd understand she wasn't afraid.

That didn't mean she wasn't mad.

"Are you nuts?" she asked Jake as she petted the big horse's neck to calm him.

Tinkerbell's hooves stamped and backed and sidled, forcing her to avoid him however she could. Her feet moved as if she were doing some kind of totally disorganized hip-hop routine.

But she stayed close to him. She couldn't let Tinkerbell panic when he was tied up this way. He could hurt himself.

"Do you really want to get me trampled?"

"Sorry," Jake said, but he didn't sound sorry.

Now Sam understood why the horse was so restless. Wisps of steam curled up from the bowl Jake carried. It smelled like hot cereal. The gelding sniffed energetically while Ace and Sweetheart did the same from their own stalls.

"Anyhow, here's a bran mash with a glug of corn oil," Jake said. He was standing behind her now, and the mash smelled good enough to remind Sam it had been hours since she'd gobbled chocolate chip cookies. "According to your gram, he'll need it every day to build him up and improve his coat."

Sam had just taken the bowl from Jake and started wondering how she was going to do this stunt, when Tinkerbell got impatient. He swung his head left, as far as the ropes allowed, knocking her back against Jake's chest.

"Ow!" she yelped, keeping her grip on the bowl. "My head! That really hurt."

"'R head?" Jake was talking again, but kind of oddly. "Ya knocked it on my chin."

Sam glanced over her shoulder to see Jake wore the close-mouthed, thoughtful look of a guy using his tongue to check for missing teeth.

"You were standing too close," Sam accused him.

"Fine, thanks," Jake managed.

"What?"

"And there's not much blood, but thanks for your sympathy."

"Oh, quit suffering."

With a sudden, muffled neigh, Tinkerbell lifted his forelegs. He rose in a frustrated half rear.

"I'll unsnap these ropes. You put that where he can get it," Jake instructed.

Sam's eyes narrowed into a glare. She would have done that in a minute. Jake just lived to order her around.

"Not a mean bone in his body," Jake said, as the gelding fell to eating.

"How do you know?" Sam demanded, even though it was true. "You've only been here five minutes. He could be an outlaw, just gaining your trust before he turns on you."

"Right," Jake replied, but then he seemed to forget her. "Chow down, fella. It's all for you."

Sam liked Jake best when he talked to horses.

He never used harsh words, but he didn't babble baby talk, either. He knew the nature of horses. Repeatedly, he'd told her horses were prey animals who only fought when they couldn't flee. But Jake knew something more. His steady voice, horseman's hands, and quiet manner convinced horses he spoke their language.

"Shoulda come in quiet," he told the gelding.

"Shouldn't have stared at you, either. But it's your turn to stare, now. I'm staying right where you can get a good look."

When the horse showed little interest, except one ear turned toward his voice, Jake placed his palm on the gelding's shoulder.

"He's a great-lookin' horse," Jake added, and it took Sam a second to realize he was talking to her.

"I know," Sam agreed. "I've got this deal with Mr. Fairchild—"

"Heard about it."

There was no sense in telling Jake he was a stuck-up know-it-all. He probably knew that, too.

"Want to buy him?" she asked.

"Don't need another horse. Witch will do," Jake said, but he stepped back a little, scanning Tinkerbell's entire body.

"I can't sell him until I figure out what he's good at," Sam said. "How would you figure out Tinkerbell's potential?"

"Tinkerbell?" Jake gave a low whistle. It didn't sound admiring. "First thing I'd do is change that fancy name."

"Yeah, he hasn't had enough trauma," Sam said sarcastically.

Jake didn't respond. In fact, he was no help at all. Still, she had to ask if he thought the vet should be called out to give Tinkerbell a checkup.

"Should I have Dr. Scott come out and look at him?"

"Your choice."

"But would you do it?" she asked. "Much as I hate to admit it, I'd like your advice."

Jake shrugged off the compliment, but he began looking Tink over.

His eyes considered the gelding's hips. Next, he stood behind the horse, close enough that if Tinkerbell struck out, his hooves wouldn't get up much momentum. Then, Jake turned his back to Sam and slid a hand over the mustang's ribs.

"Thin, but he has muscle. So I wouldn't worry about that. Still, this horse is bone-deep worried. What's his story?"

Sam didn't question Jake's intuition. He knew horses so well, she could almost believe he had telepathy.

"He's been neglected since the guy who bought him died. I think it's been a few months." She was on the verge of telling him about Mike and Ike when Jake interrupted.

"Why haven't you tended that spot on his head?"

"Let's see if you can figure that out," Sam snapped.

"It wasn't an accusation, Brat."

Sam stood with her arms crossed. If she argued, it might upset Tinkerbell. But it had, too, been an accusation.

"He is tall," Jake admitted. "Even I'd feel better if I had someone to help."

"Even you?" Sam gasped in mock surprise.

"I know you have the horse sense to help," he

added, "but you're only about five-foot two inches, right?"

Grudgingly, Sam nodded.

"This horse is . . ." Jake's voice trailed off as he measured the horse's height next to his own. "Five-foot six inches at the withers. At least. We'd both have to perch up on hay bales and that's too unsteady. I think we should wait for Ross."

"For what?" Dad's voice made all three of them turn.

"Hi, Dad." Sam watched Dad's expression. He might not say a word, but his expression would admit what a great job she'd done grooming the horse.

"He's looking good," Dad muttered. "Now, what were you waiting on?"

"Working on Tinkerbell's head where he banged it in that stupid trailer," Sam said.

"I think we could manage taking care of that without Ross," Dad told Jake. Then, after he'd studied Tinkerbell for a minute more, he added, "And we've got that old open-top trailer, which should do the trick for a short distance."

"Yeah," Sam said slowly. Dad was sure planning ahead. "But whoever buys him would probably bring their own truck. Or they could afford to rent one."

"Could, but don't want to," Dad said.

What are you talking about? Sam wanted to blurt, but she didn't.

"Are you teasing me?" she asked finally. "Because I really don't get what you're saying."

"Turns out you're some slick horse trader, Samantha," Dad said. He pushed back the brim of his Stetson and smiled. "Because you've already got a buyer for this one."

Chapter Ten

Sam tried to speak, but her lungs burned with words she didn't dare say.

I won't let him go! I have to keep him here! How can you be so happy?

Another, quieter voice whispered, *I want the Phantom to meet him.* Some instinct told her the two horses would get along. For one crazy minute, she even dreamed of releasing Tinkerbell to run wild with the Phantom's herd.

But she didn't utter a single syllable. Silence expanded and filled the barn.

Jake blurred, but she still saw the way he was rubbing the back of his neck in discomfort. Her eyes had no reason to fill with tears. Her lips parted, trembling, as she tried to make an excuse. She couldn't.

When Jake touched his hat brim and left the barn, she felt ashamed and immature. Jake hated to see her cry. If he thought she needed his help, nothing would keep him from staying beside her.

But Jake was leaving. That meant he didn't think the situation was worth her tears.

"This is what you wanted, right?" Dad asked, when Jake was gone.

"I—I—" Sam tried and still couldn't answer in anything but a stupid whimpering voice.

Dad's smile drooped and the cheer in his blue eyes faded. "You said you wanted to rescue this horse and find him a good home."

"Is it a good home?" Sam managed. It was the wrong thing to say. Dad would never sell a horse to someone he didn't trust. Her question was an insult.

"Samantha," he said, "there's just no pleasin' you."

"Dad!" Sam caught his arm before he could leave.

Dad let her stop him. He didn't look angry, just exasperated. She released her grip on his sleeve and took a deep breath.

"It's just . . . I'm getting attached to him already. I know I'm not supposed to and I know you warned me not to do it. But he's really a great horse. I didn't expect him to leave so soon."

"You're better off that he is," Dad said. "You can't adopt every stray that comes along."

"I know. And I really am glad he'll have someone

to look after him." Sam stared at Tinkerbell.

The draft horse was completely unaware that his future had changed. He only cared about finding the little bits of bran mash that had fallen into the straw. His big velvety lips sorted through his bedding, snorting every now and then as he searched.

Suddenly Sam got up the nerve to ask, "Who wants him?"

"I was down at the bank this afternoon and happened to see Mr. Martinez sittin' there behind his desk."

Mr. Martinez was a bank officer in Darton. He loved horses and rode every chance he got. He was especially fond of unusual horses, which was why he'd bought Teddy Bear, a young, curly Bashkir gelding.

"I asked him how Teddy Bear was doin' . . ." Dad began.

After he'd gotten Teddy Bear home, Mr. Martinez had discovered the horse played pranks. And tricks that might have been cute when he was a colt weren't safe once Teddy Bear was grown. So Jake had schooled him to become a well-behaved saddle horse.

"And how he was doing in this cold weather."

"With that Bashkir coat, I bet he's fine," Sam said.

"And you'd be right. He's livin' with some other horses in a pasture Martinez owns in Alkali. We got to talkin' and he told me he was looking for a big horse, maybe a Lippizaner, to add to his herd." Dad stopped and shook his head. "That man has some expensive hobbies, but it's all to your good."

"I told him about your arrangement with Duke Fairchild. I'd barely finished when he, Martinez that is, just up and offered to buy—" Dad broke off, clearly as uncomfortable with the big mustang's name as Jake was, "—him, sight unseen."

"Mr. Martinez trusts you," Sam said.

Dad shrugged one shoulder. "He said that if he could have the loan of our topless trailer, he'd drive out here tomorrow morning and load him up."

Sam couldn't help sucking in her breath. But she'd be a fool to protest, so she didn't.

"Since it was such a sudden decision," Dad went on, "I told him to keep his money for a week or two, see how things work out."

"Okay," she agreed.

She ignored the part of her heart that was clamoring for the arrangement to fail. This time last week, Tinkerbell had been abused and neglected, slated for slaughter.

If Brynna hadn't sent her to the Mineral Auction yards, no one would have noticed the calculating eyes of Baldy Harris. Mr. Martinez's wide open pasture would be paradise compared to the Dagdown stockyards.

Grow up, Sam told herself. There couldn't be a better solution.

"Before we go in," Dad said, "let's finish cleaning him up."

It was a good idea. Not only would they remove the blood from Tinkerbell's head, but Sam knew the redness from tears would have time to fade from her eyes.

Moving slowly and quietly, Dad tied Tinkerbell once more. Sam helped him clean the dried blood from Tinkerbell's poll and brush the stiffness from his mane.

With Dad watching, she cleaned the gelding's enormous hooves.

Next, Dad dampened a sponge and watched Tinkerbell lower his head so Sam could gently wipe his eyes, inside his ears, and his nostrils.

At last, Dad unsnapped the ropes so the horse could move around the box stall as he pleased. Tinkerbell's ears pricked as he listened to the wind.

Hands on hips, Dad watched and admired him.

"He's gentler than that cat of yours, isn't he?" Dad said.

"Yeah." Sam sighed. Then, she realized Dad had nodded toward a hay bale where Cougar sat, cleaning a tiger-striped paw.

When he felt Sam and Dad watching, the kitten stopped his licking. He stood, arched his back, and uttered a squeak that barely sounded feline.

Tinkerbell lowered his chin about a foot. Without blinking, he stared at the kitten. Then, his head sank level with his chest and finally almost to his knees. His breath stirred loose wisps of straw. Cougar squinted his eyes against the horse's faint exhalations, but he didn't back away. He stood on the very edge of the hay bale, unafraid.

Tinkerbell didn't move. When the two animals finally touched noses, it was the kitten who rose on his hind legs, briefly pawed the air with his front paws, and bumped the horse's nose.

Dad cleared his throat loudly. Both animals turned to stare.

"Too darn cute for me," Dad said. "Let's go eat."

Sam scooped Cougar up and held him against her chest with one hand while the other closed Tinkerbell's stall door and bolted it.

Walking toward the house lights, she nuzzled the kitten's head.

"You could have been friends," she whispered. "If only there'd been time."

Something was definitely wrong with the animals.

Overnight, two hens flew the coop. When Sam went out to feed them breakfast, the rust-colored Rhode Island Reds' feathers were fluffed and they huddled in a corner of their pen. When she did a head count, it verified her fear that two were missing.

"No." Sam moaned. "I don't have time to be the search party."

Tinkerbell only had an hour or so left on River Bend Ranch. She wanted to pet him and talk with him, maybe lead him down to the river. Instead, she hunted for the hens.

She found them in the brush beyond the barn, but it took forever.

"Go on, you crazy birds," she said, fluttering her hands to keep them moving toward their coop. "You're safer in there than you are out in the bushes."

As they scuttled before her, Sam paused to tie her sweater around her waist. She was hungry and cranky. She'd wanted to spend all morning with Tinkerbell before Mr. Martinez arrived. But she'd done the responsible thing and probably no one would even notice.

After closing the hens into their coop again, she walked out to the barn. Food could wait. A chorus of neighs floated from the barn. Ace's was the highest, followed by Sweetheart's. Tinkerbell's neigh had a low, chuckling tone that made her smile. Dallas had already fed the horses, so the greetings were for her.

"Hey, guys!" Sam called as she came from the bright morning light into the dim barn. Of course, she greeted Ace first. His head hung over the side of his stall, bobbing so that his forelock flipped up and down, hiding, then showing, his white star. He stopped when Sam drew close and cradled his chin in her hands. She kissed his nose and whispered, "Dad wants us to help move some cattle today. You'll love it."

Dad had said they'd leave right after Mr. Martinez came for Tinkerbell. He didn't say anything sentimental about taking her mind off her loss. As far as Dad was concerned, she should be celebrating. She'd made a profit with no investment except a couple hours of grooming.

Sam didn't even try to feel the same way. She knew she couldn't.

"You haven't met the others, have you?" Sam started talking as she approached Tinkerbell's stall. The horse stared at her with the gentle eyes of a much older animal. She couldn't help but think he was smart. Of course, if she told Jake that, he'd laugh and say she thought all horses were smart. "C'mon," she said, taking the lead rope from its hook. "I'll have to take you out of the barn sooner or later. We might as well have some fun first."

Tinkerbell lowered his head so that she could reach the ring of his halter. As she led him to the ten-acre pasture the other horses gathered along the fence. They looked friendlier than they had yesterday and Tinkerbell began to get excited.

Tinkerbell's stride lengthened and he broke into a trot. A trot wasn't that fast, but his legs were long and he seemed unaware of Sam's weight on the end of the rope.

Sam ran to keep up. Her right arm jerked straight up, then forward. He could dislocate it without meaning to. As her feet ran faster, her brain hoped no one was watching.

Suddenly she recognized this feeling.

She and Aunt Sue had driven to a beach south of

San Francisco several times when Sam was living there. One day she'd been waist deep in the ocean when a powerful wave rushed her off her feet and tumbled her through the nose-stinging saltwater. As it withdrew, the wave took her along. Trying to keep up with the draft horse felt just the same.

In the ocean, she'd managed to get her head up, tread water, and swim parallel to the wave's power.

Now, Sam veered left, planted her boots, braced the rope across her hips, and hung on tight.

"Easy!" she shouted, and gave the rope a jerk.

Instead of stopping, Tinkerbell swung around. Sam felt as if a bus were bearing down on her. But Tinkerbell stopped.

He faced her, blinking, and looking distressed.

Sam could almost hear him reproaching her. His expression said, *You didn't have to yell.*

"I know," Sam crooned to the big horse as she walked close and patted his shoulder. "Oh, you would have been so much fun to play with. . . ."

Sam's voice trailed off as an unfamiliar SUV rumbled across the River Bend bridge. It was teal blue and shiny with knobby off-road tires.

Blaze ran barking out to inspect the stranger.

It must be Mr. Martinez. As he pulled up next to the front porch, Sam resolved to be neighborly and grateful.

Gram had already come out of the house to talk, when Sam drew close enough to hear what they were saying.

"It's a wonderful opportunity for me," Mr. Martinez was saying, smiling.

His black hair shone under the winter sun and a small mustache danced on his upper lip. He was a little taller than Gram, and so lively he seemed not to stay still. His hands flew, illustrating his words. Watching him, Sam felt better. She had the feeling Tinkerbell wouldn't just be added to Mr. Martinez's herd of unusual horses. He would be appreciated.

Still, Sam wanted this parting to be over. Her throat felt tight and she didn't think she could trust her eyes to stay dry. With a flip of her wrist, she tethered Tinkerbell to a hitching ring.

"Hello, Mr. Martinez," Sam said. She strode toward him, palm extended for a handshake. Gram's proud smile surprised her, but she kept talking. "I'm Samantha Forster."

"Good to meet you, Samantha," he said. "What a magnificent horse you've brought me. You were incredibly farsighted to spot his potential."

Sam wondered what sort of potential Mr. Martinez was talking about as he approached Tinkerbell. Moving slowly and confidently, he talked to the animal and seemed delighted when the huge horse licked him.

"He's just like a big dog!"

"Well, not exactly," Sam said. "He nearly pulled me off my feet a minute ago."

Mr. Martinez looked at her soberly. "I won't underestimate him."

"We were talking about his name," Gram said.

"Yeah?" Sam cringed a little. She really hoped the banker wouldn't confuse the gelding with a new name.

Mr. Martinez echoed her thought.

"Your father tells me the horse has had lots of changes in his life. At first, I thought, hey, what's one more change? But Grace reminded me that, in the old days, a tinker was someone who went around house to house fixing things." He gave a satisfied nod. "I like the sound of that. So, Tinker it will stay."

Sam sighed. Everything would be all right.

But she was still sad to see him go.

Dad helped Mr. Martinez hook the trailer to his Land Rover. Brynna helped him load Tinker. Sam sat on the porch, with Blaze's head resting in her lap. She stroked the white patch on the dog's head over and over again until the trailer carried the big draft horse away, for good.

Chapter Eleven

$\mathcal{A}$ce tossed his head and pricked his ears toward the entrance to River Bend Ranch. Mr. Martinez's Land Rover had pulled Tinkerbell away about ten minutes ago and Ace was anything but sad.

"So much for you picking up my mood," Sam muttered as her horse danced, eager to get going.

"If I believed in such things, I'd say he was wishing that draft horse good riddance," Dad said.

Sam agreed. Ace was excited. As they rode south across the bridge, his eagerness kept her too busy to brood.

"Luke says he saw five of our heifers headed toward Three Ponies," Dad said, explaining why they were riding out. Luke Ely was Jake's father. If he'd said the cattle wore the River Bend brand, he was probably right.

Heifers were young cows who hadn't yet calved. They could be unpredictable.

"None of 'em should calve early," Dad added, "but you never know."

"Why wouldn't they be with the rest of the cattle?" Sam asked. Three Ponies Ranch was in the opposite direction from the winter hayracks and water tanks.

Dad shook his head. "I can't figure it out. There's still some graze down there at the lower elevation, but this range is picked bare."

Ace lifted his hooves as if each thud on the bridge boards were unexpected. As soon as they reached the other side and cut left, toward Three Ponies Ranch, Sam felt Ace's muscles bunch as if he'd bolt.

She moved her fingers, working the snaffle in his mouth, telling him he'd better pay attention, because she was.

Dad rode Jeepers-Creepers with a hackamore, and the horse moved in a classic cow horse jog, ignoring Ace's high spirits. Sam knew the Appaloosa's behavior had more to do with his rider than Jeep's temperament, so she sat a little deeper in her saddle, again signaling Ace to behave.

"There they are," Dad said. "All five together. That's handy."

Sam followed Dad's gaze.

Ace must have, too. The gelding trembled with eagerness. He might have been born a mustang, but he loved herding cattle.

Actually, he loved *chasing* cattle. When they broke from the herd, he sped to cut off every route. Eventually the cow gave up in frustration and allowed Ace to smugly escort her back to the herd.

The snow-mottled riverbank slanted down, covered in blue shadows. The heifers nosed along the slope, looking for grass that wasn't there. Ace would love charging down to retrieve them, Sam thought.

"Don't let 'em get in the river," Dad said. "It's icy cold where it's deep, and muddy where it's not. We don't need 'em bogged in mud or up to their bellies in freezing water at this stage of pregnancy. You two head 'em off."

Sam sent Ace after the heifers. Riding at an extended trot, she made a faint wave of her right hand. Although the heifers were still about a half-mile away, they responded, bounding up the bank and away from the river as if a monster were coming after them.

"What fun is that?" Sam yelped.

The heifers didn't even run in the opposite direction. Rolling their eyes, all five trotted in an orderly herd past Sam and Ace. Ace blew through his lips.

"I know, boy. It's pitiful how easily they gave up."

The heifers headed toward Dad, moving in the direction of the winter pasture.

Sam gave Ace's neck a comforting pat.

"Maybe one of them will make a break for it before we get them back down by the hayracks."

Sam made Ace wait to pursue the cattle. As soon as they passed Dad, she eased up on the reins. Ace went after them, his stride choppy and irritated. Ears up, eyes focused on the red-and-white Herefords, he fell into step with Jeepers to follow the cattle at a distance.

Dad gave her a nod. Sam knew it was the only compliment she and Ace would get. Dad wasn't surprised she'd performed the task he'd set for her. He expected her to be competent, and that was praise enough.

"The winter country isn't that far south," Dad said, continuing the conversation where he'd left off twenty minutes ago. "Shoot, you know that. You were out there yesterday with Pepper. But there's an altitude drop once you get past Alkali and head toward Darton. That means warmer temperatures and safer calving conditions, in case some of these first-time mommas have me fooled. Down there, calves have a better chance."

"You expect more snow, then?" Sam asked.

"Sure there'll be more snow," he said. "A lot of our worst weather comes in February. Now, for instance, there's a string of storms supposed to be lined up one right after the other off the coast. When they make it over those mountains, it'll be tough going for all of us. Animals and humans."

Sam felt a little embarrassed, but Dad was always tolerant of her questions because of her two-year absence. Before her accident, she'd just been a little kid. Nothing about running the ranch had meant much to her.

Now, she had a lot of catching up to do and Dad was glad to help.

"Think they'll cancel school?" Sam asked hopefully.

"It's happened," Dad said. "No telling if it will this time. Brynna was online on her computer at the office yesterday, tryin' to see when they might strike. The experts give 'em two or three days." Dad's smile was half admiration, half confusion. "Doesn't feel to me like one will hit anytime soon, but I'm thinking with my bones."

Cutting cross-country on horseback instead of driving the truck as they had yesterday actually seemed to make the trip to winter pasture quicker. Still, it took over an hour.

Now, two or three miles ahead, Sam could see a couple hayracks that stood about a city block apart. To Sam, the movements around them were just dark shapes of animals, but the heifers recognized their herd. As if they hadn't left of their own free will, the heifers rocked into a joyous run toward home.

"We dropped off more feed this morning," Dad said. His stiff tone warned Sam what was coming next. "We didn't see any horses, but Pepper said you did yesterday."

Sam's mind raced. She couldn't think of one thing she could say that would improve Dad's prickly attitude, but she didn't want him to think she hadn't heard.

"Yeah," she replied.

"I'm not going to have mustangs eating feed that's intended for cattle. You know that, don't you?"

"Uh-huh."

"If a big storm sweeps in, that hay will make the difference between life and death. We all depend on those cattle to get fat, go to market, and keep this ranch afloat."

Sam knew Dad was right, but what about the horses? She couldn't bear the thought that mustangs could starve while the cows grew fat.

As they rode, the dark shapes ahead became more distinct. Some of them were mustangs. She was sure of it. She sucked in a breath as one, surrounded by bored-looking cattle, pulled hay from the nearest rack.

At the next rack, farther on, she was pretty sure the horses and cattle were feeding together.

Oh, no. Dad's attitude was due to get a whole lot worse, as soon as he quit lecturing her and focused on what lay ahead.

"Are you listening?" Dad asked.

"I know."

"You know what?"

"I mean, yes," Sam said, and her edgy tone made Dad rise in his stirrups and squint.

"They're back." Dad shook his head. "Samantha, here's where you show what you're made of. We're going to chase those horses away from the hay and we're going to make it darned unpleasant for them, so they don't come back."

Sam didn't ask what he meant. When he urged Jeep into a gallop, Ace followed.

Leave now. Sam fixed her eyes on the horses, hoping they sensed her silent warning. *He won't hurt you if you go.*

The mustangs' heads flew up. Hay dropped to the cold desert floor as they began backing, whirling, bumping cattle, and scattering along with them. The chaos was silent, almost like a pantomime. Only the hammering hooves of riders, bearing down on the animals, broke the winter calm.

Then Dad gave a yipping call she hadn't heard since that first cattle drive, when he was helping to turn a stampede. Did the cattle and horses mistake it for a coyote, or was it just a sound so alien that it scared them?

Sam didn't know that answer. But she did know that that stampede had been her fault, just as this confrontation was. She wasn't being paranoid. She knew it was her fault, because there stood the Phantom. And he was holding his ground.

Her moonlight-colored stallion was in disguise. Winter made him resemble a medieval unicorn. Silken hair fringed the underside of his head from chin to throat. Sunlight sparkled there as he jerked his head skyward, calling his mares to him.

Zanzibar, go! Using the stallion's secret name, Sam sent him all the urgency her thoughts could hold, but the horse had recognized her and he felt safe.

He snorted and stamped. Ice splintered and flew like sparks from his hooves.

He lowered his head and swept his muzzle just inches from the ground. Steam jetted from his nostrils and his brown eyes peered up at her. They flashed with mischief from behind his heavy forelock.

They'd played this game when he was a colt. Blackie, she'd called him then, because he'd been night black with no socks, no star, no flash of white anywhere. The first time they'd played this game, a sweater she'd tied around her waist had loosened and dropped. With one swoop of his head and snap of his teeth, he'd plucked it from the ground and held it high.

"We can't play, boy," she whispered to the stallion. "Not now."

She felt as if something heavy were crushing her chest. She knew how rare it was, to have a wild stallion for a friend. But if she played with him now, it would only make their parting worse.

Pulling her gaze away from him, Sam realized

Dad had galloped past the disturbed horses to regather the cattle. Quietly, holding Jeep to a flat-footed walk, he escorted them back to the hayracks. Maybe he'd leave the Phantom's herd alone.

"You've gotta go, boy," Sam told the Phantom. "Now, while he's busy."

But the stallion loved her voice.

Snowflakes floated from his mane like confetti as he left his mares to prance forward and touch noses with Ace.

He was so close. Sam's fingers trembled. She could touch him if she wanted.

But right now, he was exchanging snorts and nickers with Ace.

The two horses were friends. Once they'd been companions on the high green mesas and white desert playas. Neither had forgotten.

They were only quiet for a few seconds. The loud squeals, kicks, and nips following their greeting composed a ritual as old as horses. Because she'd felt it coming, Sam rode it out, easily.

Suddenly, the Phantom froze in place, ears pointing past her.

Leaning low on Jeep's neck, Dad galloped at the mares. He had to have done it to draw the Phantom's attention. Dad knew horses. He knew it was a challenge no stallion could ignore. The Phantom ran to meet him. Ears pinned, legs flying straight forward, then back, then straight, he closed the distance to his mares seconds before Jeep reached them.

Head low in a snaking, herding motion, the Phantom nipped and slashed, teeth clacking, but never touching the fleeing mares. They ran for the cleft between the hills.

For one second, a dappled mare seemed to guide the others. Sam hoped the Phantom had a new lead mare. But then the mare was surrounded by the other mustangs and Sam could tell it was the stallion's fury, coming up behind, that kept them all running.

Dad didn't chase them far. No more than a quarter-mile into the chase, he turned Jeep in a slow curve to the left. The Appaloosa slowed as he approached Sam and Ace.

By the time she could see Dad's expression, Jeep had settled into a jog once more. Silently, Sam waited for Dad. As she sat there, her quiet hands and legs told Ace that everything was just fine. But her mind was a tangle of wild thoughts. The Phantom didn't know he needed her, but he did.

She thought again of the story she'd told Tinkerbell, about the lion and the mouse. She and the stallion shared a bond and he could use her help to keep his herd safe and healthy, even if he didn't know it.

But what would she say to Dad?

They were both angry. They both believed they were right. They were both stubborn. What would be the point in talking?

So they didn't.

Dad sent Jeep toward home. Head high, nostrils flared in exhilaration, Ace jogged beside him.

Sam's glance slid sideways to Dad. She wanted to believe he'd reached the same conclusion she had: there was nothing to talk about. But Dad's darkly tanned face was carved with disappointment.

Here's where you show what you're made of, he'd said, but she hadn't ridden beside him, hadn't chased the wild horses away from the hay, hadn't chosen Dad over the Phantom.

With a squeak of leather, Dad straightened in the saddle. His mouth flattened in a hard, straight line. His chin jerked up, eyelids lowered, and Sam knew she would pay for this decision.

Two hours later, after they'd cooled and brushed their horses in total silence, Dad and Sam headed for the house.

"I made an early dinner," Gram said as Sam came in ahead of Dad.

"And I," Brynna added as she dangled a pink bakery box from its strings, "have chocolate cake from Clara's Diner."

"I have business over at the Kenworthys'," Dad said, leaning his head in the kitchen door. Each word was quieter, as if he were reconsidering.

Maybe it was Gram's crestfallen look, or the smell of hamburgers. Maybe it was the prospect of chocolate cake. Something changed Dad's mind.

"It can wait 'til we've eaten," he said, then climbed the stairs to wash up without another word.

"Were the cattle all right?" Gram asked, looking after him.

"Just fine," Sam said. "We found the heifers right away and got them back to winter pasture."

She didn't see any reason to mention the mustangs.

"Your father's as touchy as every other creature around here," Gram said, turning back to the stove. "Wonder what's gotten into them all."

"Some people would blame it on the change in barometric pressure that comes along with a storm," Brynna said. "But that doesn't sound right to me."

Brynna was usually right about scientific things. This time she was definitely right. Dad's bad mood had nothing to do with a change in the weather and everything to do with mustangs.

But Sam kept quiet. Both women shrugged, and dinner was on the table in minutes. Hamburgers on yeasty homemade buns, home fries made from real potatoes, a green salad decorated with carrot curls, and chocolate cake for dessert was Sam's all-time favorite meal. In spite of the tension that radiated off Dad, she enjoyed every bite because she'd just realized the Phantom wouldn't be mad at her.

The Phantom had seen Dad and Jeep as rivals for his herd. It was a challenge he, as a herd stallion, had faced often. He wouldn't resent her, wouldn't settle back into that awful confusion he'd felt after he'd been captured and forced to buck in the rodeo.

Dad ate, nodding his appreciation at Gram, but he didn't relax. His knuckles were white from gripping his fork way too tight. Sam knew it was because he was mad at her, because she wasn't mad at the mustangs. Now she sort of wished he'd gone ahead over to the Kenworthys' house.

Still, Sam took silent advice from Gram, who'd learned to wait Dad out. He usually worked off anger by rearranging hay bales in the loft of the barn, or waxing his truck, or rubbing neat's-foot oil into an old halter.

So, Sam studied her fries, looking for the crunchiest one. She felt more and more confident that the day wouldn't be a total disaster.

But she hadn't counted on Brynna.

Brynna didn't blurt out a question or demand to know what was wrong, but her curiosity was obvious. Twice, her eyes caught Sam's. Both times, Sam had started to send some kind of signal, when she noticed Dad watching her and had to shrug as if nothing was wrong.

If they could only get through dinner without a blowup, Dad would leave and have some thinking time in his truck. Sam would call Jen immediately or go up to her room and read the new mystery novel Aunt Sue had sent as an early Valentine's Day gift. One thing she wouldn't do was give Brynna and

Gram a chance to pry the truth out of her.

Sam knew their loyalties would be divided. Gram would think Dad was right to favor the cattle over the wild horses. Brynna would believe a balance should be reached.

Halfway through his slice of cake, Dad put down his fork.

Smiling, Brynna asked, "Ready to tell us what happened?"

"What's happened is, this cussed adopt-a-nag program doesn't work."

Dad had to be talking about the BLM's mustang adoption program. Didn't he know the way he'd mentioned it sounded like a dare?

Brynna lay her fork down as well. "Really?"

Sam's pulse beat hard in her wrists and temples. Brynna sounded entirely too calm. She should have jumped right into lecturing Dad about the adoption program.

"You bring in a lot of young, good-looking horses and leave genetic duds out on the range," Dad said.

How could he say that when the Phantom and Moon and dozens of other beautiful horses still ran free?

Brynna leaned back in her chair. She tossed the tail of her red braid back over one shoulder and crossed her arms. Clearly, she was unhappy, but she didn't stop Dad.

"Go on," she told him.

"Do you know I heard of a whole band of blind horses in Utah? I have to pay for every cow and calf that eats a blade of grass — or not, because cattle don't paw out plant roots like horses — and those useless horses are out there running on public lands for free!" Dad pushed his chair away from the table. "There's no sense in that."

Sam knew Brynna had a blind mustang mare named Penny she rode around the Willow Springs corrals. Brynna loved that mare, and Dad hadn't shown very good judgment in bringing up blind horses.

Brynna's face matched her red hair. Was she holding her breath while Dad ranted? Why wasn't Brynna saying anything? Was she so eager to avoid a fight with her new husband that she'd let him say whatever he wanted about the program she'd devoted most of her working life to building?

I sure wouldn't be quiet, Sam thought. *Some things are worth standing up for.*

"Maybe we should have this talk in the other room while Sam does the dishes," Gram suggested.

That sounded good to Sam. If Brynna kept skirting the issue and being polite, Sam knew *she'd* defend the horses. And that wouldn't work. Dad was already mad at her.

"There's nothing to talk about," Dad said.

Finally, Brynna spoke up.

"Are you content to make up your mind without a

civilized discussion?" Brynna asked Dad. Her tone was level.

I could learn something from her, Sam thought. Brynna had a different approach than Gram, but she might just calm Dad down.

Sam took another bite of cake, but she'd barely swallowed when Dad went off again.

"I don't need to discuss what I saw with my own eyes, and that was horses, driving cattle off from the hay I broke my back to sow, tend, and harvest."

"Driving them away?" Brynna asked.

Sam guessed Dad thought that was what he'd seen, but he was wrong. Horses had been standing alongside cattle at one hayrack. At another, the cattle acted bored, as if they'd already eaten their fill.

When Brynna's eyes darted across the table, Sam shook her head.

"Don't go askin' her," Dad snapped. "A girl who'd—" He broke off, shaking his head.

"Who'd what?" Gram demanded. "Wyatt?"

"Let her explain, if she can," Dad said. He stood, holding his napkin balled up in one fist. "'Cause I sure don't understand it. I thought she was growin' up, learnin' to find solutions for things she wanted changed. Takin' that photograph to prove the white stud wasn't the one stealin' mares, for instance. And helping to track him down at the rodeos, even convincing Trudy Allen to open that home for wild horses. But now, she thinks I should let them starve my cattle. I just don't know."

Dad dropped the napkin on the table. He walked out, leaving the kitchen door open as he went onto the porch. Cold air wafted into the kitchen as he shrugged into his heavy coat.

"One thing I do know," he added, over his shoulder, "is why some ranchers guard their cattle with rifles."

Gram gasped.

Brynna shot to her feet and rounded the table, motioning Sam and Gram to stay put.

Sam stayed at the table, but her thoughts tumbled one over the other. Dad couldn't mean that the way it sounded. She knew he'd never shoot a horse. All the same, he shouldn't have said it.

Brynna didn't look so understanding anymore. Not only was her face flushed, her neck was red all the way down into the collar of her khaki uniform shirt.

"I don't want to hear about rifles. We're not there yet," Brynna told Dad. "When we are, you let me know and something will be done. Until then? You know a few mouthfuls of hay aren't worth doing jail time."

Was that a threat? Sam didn't think so, but part of Brynna's job as an employee of the U.S. government was assuring no one harmed or harassed wild horses. Maybe she was just reminding him.

Dad left the porch. The screen door didn't slam

behind him. He didn't turn on the yard lights, but Sam heard his boots take each sure step.

Sam watched Brynna bite her lip. Clearly, she wanted to go after him, but she didn't. She knew he was wrong.

Sam listened. The soles of Dad's boots crunched on the gravel driveway as he headed for his truck, and then he stopped.

"Samantha." Dad didn't yell, but she heard him quite clearly.

Brynna stepped out of Sam's way. As she moved after Dad, Sam almost stumbled on Cougar.

"No way," she muttered. She grabbed up the kitten. "I'm not letting you out there to be coyote bait."

As she shut the kitten on the other side of the screen door, Sam heard something else. A single set of hoofbeats.

What if Ace . . . ? What if the Phantom . . . ?

Before she could imagine much of anything, Sam stepped into the dark ranch yard and gasped.

Tinkerbell had returned.

Chapter Twelve

Not only had Tinkerbell returned, he was inside the ten-acre pasture.

Inside?

"What's he doing here?" Sam asked. "How did he get in?"

"I wouldn't know," Dad said.

By this time, Gram and Brynna had joined them.

"He sure looks proud of himself," Gram said, as the big horse hung his head over the fence to be petted. "Should we call Mr. Martinez?"

"Time enough for that in the morning," Dad said. "It's not like the horse is bought and paid for. Martinez may change his mind if this gelding won't stay put."

Oh, no. Mr. Martinez had to keep him.

Suddenly, Sam felt sick. Just last night she'd been wishing Mr. Martinez didn't want Tinkerbell. *Be careful what you wish for; you just might get it.* Sam didn't know where she'd heard that saying, but now it made awful sense.

She'd wished to have Tinkerbell back and here he was. But if no one else wanted him and he had to go back up for auction, she knew Baldy Harris would be there to bid on him for the Dagdown Packing Company.

"If he's come all that way on his own, he's run about fifteen miles," Dad said, taking his truck keys from his pocket. "Might want to bring him out and look him over."

Sam watched Dad walk to his truck, but her mind was already suggesting ways Tinkerbell could have hurt himself. He could have abraded his legs by leaping over wooden fence rails. He could have pulled a tendon from overuse and if he fell, he could be peppered with gravel bruises from rough terrain. That injury to his poll could have been aggravated by a fifteen-mile run, too.

As Dad drove away, Sam stood at the gate to the ten-acre corral. She'd seen a horse in pain before, and Tinkerbell didn't have that look. But dusk could hide all kinds of injuries. She needed to get him inside the barn, under the lights.

As she unbolted the gate, Tinkerbell's head lifted.

He watched her with a hopeful look. Sam felt flattered. Maybe she was part of what brought him back to River Bend.

Tinkerbell came right through the gate, nuzzled Sam's neck, and stood still while Brynna snapped a lead rope on his halter.

"Is he shod?" she asked as they walked toward the barn.

Sam's mind replayed the moments in the barn with Dad, when she'd cleaned the gelding's huge hooves. "Yes, why?"

"I was always taught you didn't turn out a shod horse in a halter, because he might use a hind leg to scratch his face, catch his hoof, go down, and break a leg." Brynna paused. Together, she and Sam stared at the massive animal. To perform such an action, he'd have to be a contortionist. "On the other hand," Brynna went on, "I don't think he'd try that, do you?"

As they reached the barn door, Tinkerbell stopped.

Brynna smooched to the horse and gave the lead rope a tug. "C'mon, big boy."

The gelding stayed put.

"Did something happen in there yesterday?" Brynna asked.

"Ace was acting jealous and pretending he was going to bite," Sam said. "And the sound of the wind through the barn seemed to worry him."

"Why don't you go ahead and have a talk with

Ace and we'll be along in a second," Brynna said.

Ace was already on alert. He'd heard the draft horse approaching and his ears were pinned back in warning.

"You knock that off," Sam scolded. She reached up to pet his nose and Ace pulled away. "You know I like you best."

Her voice might have been the whining of a bug for all the attention Ace paid her.

"Sam, this is one nervous horse," Brynna said. She was barely in control as she and Tinkerbell came through the barn door. His steps were each a different length and Brynna had trouble keeping up. "He's sure Ace isn't pretending. And if a horse this big is afraid Ace wants to take a hunk out of him, he's probably right.

"I think I can hold him, but if they start to go at it," Brynna warned, "just get out of the way."

Sam nodded, then turned back to Ace. "You are a spoiled brat," Sam told him, but it didn't appear to hurt the gelding's feelings. His little Arab-shaped face quivered from ears to muzzle as he watched the draft horse step into the box stall and sigh.

Under the barn's fluorescent lights, Brynna examined Tink.

"This is the first time I've had a real chance to see him, Sam. You made a good decision. He was well worth saving." Brynna's eyes darted to one side, glancing back toward the house. Sam wondered if she was recalling the fight she'd just had with Dad.

Sam knew things probably weren't as bad as they felt right now. Everything wasn't falling apart, but she wished level-headed Jen was here to tell her so.

The cattle were scattered all over the place and they might lose some calves. Dad wanted to get rid of the Phantom's herd. Tinkerbell wasn't where he was supposed to be. Mr. Martinez might not want him anymore. And Dad and Brynna had had their first real fight.

Jen's logical mind and knowledge of animals would come in handy right now. But Brynna was the next best thing.

"How do you think he got here?" Sam blurted. "I mean, out of one pasture and into another."

"Our fences are just about four feet tall," Brynna mused.

"Do you think he can jump that high?" Sam asked. Looking at the huge horse, it was hard to believe he could lift hundreds of pounds of bone and muscle over a four-foot fence. Twice.

"Is there any other explanation?" Brynna asked. "Nothing else makes sense."

Sam felt her spirits lift, slightly. "If he could jump, it would make him a much more valuable horse. I mean, just in case Mr. Martinez doesn't want him now."

Brynna stood near Tinkerbell's head and the big brown gelding licked her palm just as he had Sam's.

"You're pretty sweet for a fugitive," Brynna told him.

"How can we find out if he's a jumper?" Sam asked.

Her few jumps on Ace had been unintentional. The feeling had been thrilling, but half the thrill was fear.

The idea of riding Tinkerbell, being perched nearly six feet in the air atop his back, was scary enough. She didn't have the nerve to ride him at a jump.

"Call Katie Sterling at Sterling Stables," Brynna suggested. "She trains show jumpers. She'd know where to start."

Once, Sam had made the mistake of going horse shopping with Rachel Slocum. One of the places they'd visited had been Sterling Stables and Sam had liked Katie Sterling a lot.

Then, Sam had a better idea.

"Ryan Slocum," Sam said thoughtfully.

"That's right!" Brynna said. "Back when Linc was trying to buy the Phantom, he told me he wanted a jumper for his son."

It was the perfect solution. Ryan was only a couple of miles away. The Slocums had a covered arena. And Ryan would know how to test Tinkerbell's jumping skills.

The only awkward part—and it was really awkward—was calling Gold Dust Ranch. What if Rachel answered the phone? The girl hated her, and Sam hadn't made it any better when she'd been sarcastic to her this morning. Rachel had probably been gossiping about her, too. Even if Rachel didn't say something catty or cruel when Sam called, she might not call Ryan to the phone.

And Linc Slocum . . . Sam cringed. He'd think she had a crush on Ryan, and Sam couldn't predict how he'd handle that. Would he jeer that she didn't have a chance with a guy so far above her, socially? Or would he see Sam as a shortcut to being western — just as he did a fine horse or a trophy belt buckle? If so, he'd be yodeling his discovery all over town and Sam couldn't stand that.

Jen really did have a crush on Ryan and she'd probably welcome an excuse to talk with him, but Sam was pretty sure Jen wouldn't feel comfortable just wandering up to the mansion from the foreman's house to tell Ryan that Sam wanted him to call.

"Call Helen Coley," Brynna said.

"Huh?" Sam snapped out of staring at the barn wall. Brynna must have been watching and reading her mind. "Mrs. Coley?"

Helen Coley was the Slocums' housekeeper. She was also a talented seamstress and a great admirer of wild horses.

"Sure," Brynna said. "When she was working on my wedding gown, she gave me the phone number for her private line."

"If I told her about Tinkerbell—"

"I know she'd get Ryan to call you," Brynna finished.

Sam glanced at her watch. It was early enough that they might be able to work something out for tomorrow. Tomorrow was Sunday and she did have homework, but Tinkerbell's safety was more important.

"Come up with any ideas for your community service project?" Brynna asked suddenly.

"No," Sam said. "And Mrs. Santos wants me to work on it with Rachel Slocum."

Brynna took a deep breath. "You two don't have a lot in common, but I'm sure you can come up with something great." Brynna's face took on an impish look and she lowered her voice to a whisper. "With her money and your imagination . . ."

Sam laughed. Brynna was really nice, and she was fun. For a minute, Sam wanted to tell Brynna that the real problem wasn't selecting a topic; it was making a presentation to the student council.

But Brynna would probably dismiss her problem as nerves. And nerves seemed like a frivolous, silly concern compared to calves that might freeze, horses that might starve, and a fresh disagreement with Dad.

Besides, Brynna might not understand. She did lots of public speaking in her job. She'd even flown to Washington, D.C. to present the mustangs' cause to a Senate subcommittee.

I might be able to do that, it suddenly occurred to Sam.

Standing in front of the student council, talking to those popular kids, might not be so terrifying if she were explaining something she cared about.

"What I'd really like to do is something for the wild horses," Sam suggested.

Brynna paused in her inspection of Tinkerbell and her blue eyes focused on Sam. "You're not worrying about what your Dad was saying, are you?" she asked.

It was quiet for a minute. Sam heard only the rustling of hooves in the straw as she thought about what Dad had said.

He hadn't meant that remark about shooting the horses. She knew that for sure. Dad was frustrated because he felt helpless. Everything he cared about — his work, his home, his ability to live the life he loved — was tied up with those cattle, and he thought the horses were endangering them.

Tinkerbell tensed, then stared at the barn door as if he expected company. Sam shook off her trance.

"I am sort of worried," Sam admitted. "I mean, I saw the horses going after our hay and I don't blame Dad for being mad, but I don't blame the horses, either. They're hungry."

Brynna gave a heartfelt sigh. "So are the coyotes, cougars, and bobcats. That's what makes it dangerous for the horses, especially the mares in foal. It's tough for them to slog through deep snow and the predators know it.

"Some won't make it," Brynna continued. "It's a hard life being a wild animal, taking shelter from storms under trees, against rocks. Even when the weather is clear, this is a searching time for the mustangs," she said. "Winter has lasted for months and spring hasn't begun to green things up yet. In a lot of places, it's so cold they can't paw through to the remaining grass. We used to do hay drops," Brynna said wistfully.

Sam imagined airplanes flying above the snowy range, then opening some kind of doors in the bellies of the aircraft. Instead of dropping bombs, they'd drop golden, life-giving hay.

"Wow, that's a great idea. They'd have hay of their own and the ranchers wouldn't be mad at them. Why did you stop?"

"Money," Brynna said. "BLM is a federal bureau and the current administration in Washington has cut funds for wildlife. They're just not a priority."

Brynna closed the door to Tinkerbell's box stall and started out of the barn. Sam walked beside her, thinking.

"A lot of people like wild horses," Sam insisted. "Even people who live far away—in Florida, Virginia, Canada—you know, all over the place. Wouldn't they help the horses if they could?"

"They might, but the government doesn't work

that way." Brynna shook her head. "Still, it's worth thinking about. I wouldn't be surprised if you came up with something." Brynna's arm swept around Sam's shoulders and squeezed. "You are one smart cookie, Samantha Forster, and I'm glad to be in your family."

Sam was grinning as she shouted "good night" to the horses.

Brynna turned off the barn light. They were about to walk back to the house when something made Sam stop. Just as the lights dimmed out she'd seen something out of the ordinary.

"Wait a minute." She walked back into the barn, flipped the light switch, and beckoned Brynna to return. "Look," she said, pointing.

Tinkerbell wasn't alone in his stall.

Cougar was with him. The tiny tiger-striped kitten was curled up, tail fluffed to cover and warm his nose, sleeping right in the middle of Tinkerbell's broad bay back.

Chapter Thirteen

Back inside the house, Sam scarfed down another piece of chocolate cake to fortify herself for what she had to do next. Brynna insisted Sam should call Mr. Martinez and tell him about Tinkerbell's escape before she called Ryan.

After her last bite, Sam stood. Still holding her empty plate, she took the dishwashing soap from its shelf.

"You're stalling," Brynna said. "I'll wash your plate while you call."

"I don't know his number."

"We have a phone book," Brynna told her.

"It might be too late," Sam said.

"It's perfectly appropriate to call an adult at eight

o'clock on a Saturday night."

"But I'm kind of scared to call Mr. Martinez," Sam protested. "I mean, Dad's the one who made the arrangements in the first place."

"Sam," Brynna said in a cautioning tone. "Remember what your Dad said about making things happen instead of just wishing they would?"

"I heard him," Sam said. She flipped through the phone book instead of meeting Brynna's eyes. Even after she found Mr. Martinez's number, she kept looking down.

"Well, he's right."

"I know." Sam sighed heavily and began dialing.

Mr. Martinez reported Tinkerbell had unloaded as easily as he'd loaded. He'd touched noses with Teddy Bear, then began grazing among the other horses shortly after entering the pasture.

"All in all," Mr. Martinez said, "I think things will work out fine."

Mr. Martinez's tone was pleasant, but he was clearly puzzled by her call.

"The thing is," Sam said, "Tinkerbell is here." She closed her eyes and waited.

"There? There at River Bend?"

"He just showed up. About an hour ago."

"He came on his own?" Mr. Martinez asked.

"He must have," Sam said. She held a hand over her closed eyes. She didn't know exactly why. "We were pretty surprised to find him."

It was quiet long enough that Sam heard classical music playing at Mr. Martinez's house. As violins soared, Sam pictured an elegant house with crystal goblets and softly glowing candles. Runaway horses probably didn't belong in Mr. Martinez's life.

"That's a long distance," Mr. Martinez mused. "He's safe, though?"

Sam opened her eyes. Mr. Martinez was more concerned about Tinkerbell's welfare than the trouble the big horse had caused. If Tinkerbell had only stayed put, Mr. Martinez would have given him the affection he deserved.

"He's fine," Sam said. "Brynna and I just looked him over inch by inch."

"And so . . ." This time it was Mr. Martinez who sighed. "You are calling to see if I still want him. Is that it?"

Sam couldn't admit it. "I just thought you should know," she said, instead.

"Thank you," he said. "This may change my decision. Of course you know that. But I'd like the chance to go out and check the pasture fence. If there was a section down, it would be natural for him to find his way back to you."

Sam bit her lip. Why hadn't she thought of that?

"Do you want me to call Clara? The diner's so close to your pasture she could go check the fence."

"I'll call, Samantha. And if you'll give me a couple days to think about it, I'll get back to you about Tinker's future."

Tinker's future. The words had an ominous sound.

"Okay," Sam said. She cleared her throat, trying to cover the fear in her voice.

"We won't let anything awful happen to him, you and I," Mr. Martinez promised. "Something will work out."

"Thanks, Mr. Martinez," she said. "Take your time."

Sam hung up and left her hand on the telephone receiver.

"Is it still Saturday night?" Sam asked as she looked up and saw Brynna studying her.

Brynna nodded. "Feel like you've just run fifteen miles yourself?"

"Kind of," Sam admitted as she dialed Mrs. Coley's number. "But now it should feel easy talking to Ryan."

Only five minutes passed between the time Sam talked with Mrs. Coley and the time Ryan Slocum called back. He sounded excited about working with a heavy hunter prospect. He'd done it before in England, riding a Friesian mare over jumps. He could barely wait to get started with Tinkerbell.

"I'll prepare the arena first thing and be ready as early as you can get here," he promised. "Shall we say nine? And don't worry about tack. I'll cobble something together that should suit our purposes."

"Thanks so much," Sam said, and hung up. Brynna had stood at her elbow listening the entire time, so

Sam didn't have to explain.

"Great! I'll drive you over in the morning," Brynna said, but then her eyes widened. "One problem, though. The trailer."

"Oh, yeah," Sam said.

Why had it taken them both so long to realize they had no way to transport Tinkerbell to Gold Dust Ranch? Mr. Martinez still had their open horse trailer.

Brynna and Sam sat at the kitchen table, staring at each other.

"For some reason, it doesn't feel like a good idea to call him back. Mr. Martinez, I mean, while he's still deciding about Tinkerbell," Sam said, and Brynna nodded in understanding. "We could pony him over there," Sam suggested.

"Maybe." Brynna's voice was dubious. "If we led Tinkerbell between two horses, which ones do you think we should use? Tank and . . ."

"No, it's a dumb idea. Never mind," Sam said. "The other horses are starting to like him, but that might be pushing them too fast." Sam looked down at the sound of Cougar batting his paw against the edge of the kitchen door. He'd been seeking an escape route since she had brought him back inside. If they had a horse who felt the same about Tinkerbell as the kitten did, they'd be set. But they didn't.

They still had no solution when Dad came home from the Kenworthys' house. He entered talking.

"Winter used to be a quiet time," he said. "Not this year. Between the cattle and horses spread from here to breakfast and this"—Dad bent to scoop up Cougar—"feline fugitive, I don't know what to think."

Dad closed the door and deposited Cougar on Sam's lap.

Was Dad happier or just preoccupied? When he rumpled her hair and kissed Brynna, Sam decided it didn't matter which.

Then, he seemed to hear the silence. "What's wrong with you two?"

Brynna told him their plan.

Dad's raised eyebrows said he thought it was a silly idea, but Brynna wore an "I-dare-you" look. Dad must have recognized it, because he offered a suggestion instead of criticism.

"The Elys have a cattle truck that'd work. Get Jake to drive Sam over," Dad said to Brynna, "and I might just make you a real Sunday breakfast."

Brynna flashed Sam a look that said she couldn't refuse. Dad knew the family was divided on the issue of wild horses. This was his way of saying he didn't want the disagreement to escalate into a civil war.

But Jake and Ryan were not a good combination.

"Call him, Sam," Brynna urged. She dialed and handed Sam the phone. "Here."

Sam wanted to ask Brynna to quit rushing her into things, but the phone was already ringing.

Maybe no one would be home. It was Saturday night, after all.

The phone was still ringing at the Elys' when Dad and Brynna left the kitchen to go watch television with Gram.

Jake and Ryan didn't hate each other. In fact, Ryan pretended not to notice Jake, but Jake couldn't stand Ryan's British accent and exacting manners.

She was just about to hang up, when Nate, the oldest Ely brother, answered. Grudgingly, he gave the phone to Jake.

"Jake, Tinkerbell is back. It seems like he jumped out of Mr. Martinez's corral and ran all the way back to River Bend. We found him in the ten-acre pasture a couple hours ago."

"Huh," Jake said.

Anyone else would voice astonishment, but not Jake. Sam wasn't surprised by his seeming acceptance of Tinkerbell's stunt. She knew if she told Jake that it appeared Tinkerbell had sprouted wings in the vicinity of his withers, Jake would react the same way.

"Since Mr. Martinez isn't sure he wants to keep Tinkerbell, I want to see if he really can jump. We're just guessing that he can."

"Yeah," Jake said.

Sam took the syllable as encouragement to keep talking, but here came the hard part. "So, I want to take him over to the Gold Dust Ranch. Ryan has done some jumping and he said he'd put Tinker through his paces and see what he could do."

"You already talked to him?"

"Mr. Martinez?" Sam asked, puzzled. "Sure."

"No," Jake said.

Sam bristled, but she didn't need to irritate Jake when she was asking for his help.

"Oh, you mean Ryan? Yes, he said he'd be glad to do it, and I'm thinking that if Tinkerbell can jump, I might have an easier time finding him a good home. And since Mr. Martinez still has our trailer, my dad thought you might be willing to drive Tinkerbell over in your cattle truck. With me, too, of course."

Having said all she could to convince him, Sam waited.

There was a moment of silence, but then Jake agreed. Of course he had to make it seem like he was doing Dad a favor, not her.

"I'm always willing to help Wyatt and, if nothin' else, it'll be amusin'," he drawled.

The next morning, Sam stood in the ranch yard holding Tinkerbell's lead rope while Gram, dressed for church in a navy-blue dress and matching gloves, played with the big horse.

In spite of the foam and alfalfa clinging to his lips, she let Tinkerbell sniff her gloves.

"Not the usual hands, are they?" she joked, then turned to Sam. "I can't help loving this animal. He has so much personality. Look how those big brown eyes sparkle."

As soon as Gram had driven her big yellow Buick across the bridge, Jake pulled in driving a cattle truck that had seen better days.

He looked nice, as if he were going to church, too.

Sam was about to compliment him when he brushed by her, lowered the truck's tailgate, and grumbled, "Let's get this done."

Keeping her compliments to herself, Sam led Tinkerbell up the ramp. He seemed almost eager to get inside.

"I've gotta be home by noon," Jake said, as if Sam weren't moving fast enough. "My dad wants me to crawl under the house and wrap insulation around the pipes."

Sam shivered. Wiggling into the narrow space under a house in this freezing cold weather made her chores sound pleasant, but Sam didn't sympathize with Jake. At least not aloud. She just kept talking to Tinkerbell, helping him settle into the new setting.

"You are such a good boy," Sam told the gelding just before she left the rear of the truck. Then, to Jake, she said, "He acts like he does it every day."

Jake shrugged. "Been three days in a row, hasn't it?"

"Yes," Sam said, climbing into the passenger's seat. "But still."

As Jake made a right turn off the main road and

headed toward Gold Dust Ranch, he warned her, "I'm just the driver. Don't be expecting me to socialize."

Sam turned in her seat and considered Jake. He wore fresh jeans and a brick-colored shirt with pearl snaps. His hair still smelled of shampoo. He *looked* ready to socialize. If she said that, though, it would be just like Jake to turn around and drive home again.

For the first time, Sam wondered if she'd heard something else beneath Jake's dislike for Ryan. Shyness and uncertainty?

It made sense, she thought. Jake was basically shy. He spoke little to friends and was always uneasy around strangers. He'd spent most of his life in this quiet corner of Nevada.

Ryan, on the other hand, had shown a lively, open charm from the first time Sam had met him. Had living in Europe given him a knack at fitting in, or had he always been that way?

Sam couldn't guess, but she could see how Jake would be ill at ease around him. Suddenly, thoughts of Jake's shyness led her to a problem of her own.

"I guess you've already started your community service project," Sam hinted.

"I guess so," Jake said. "Everyone has." He drove along a minute or two, then added, "Right?"

Sam didn't answer him directly. Instead she asked another question. "Since you're, you know, not the most talkative guy around, how did it go when you had to present your idea to the student council?"

"I don't know. I just did it. Well, Brian and me. After we saw the graffiti spray-painted on the tribal museum, we wanted to do something." Jake shrugged. "That place means a lot to my grandfather. Since Dad would definitely yank my license away if I got into a fight—"

"A fight?" Sam asked.

"We were going to find the guys who did it." Jake raised his chin and smiled. "But doing the graffiti patrol thing was a way to make Grandfather happy and get the stupid requirement filled."

As Sam mulled over what Jake had said, she glanced toward Lost Canyon. There wasn't a mustang in sight.

"Hey," Jake said, and there was a suspicious edge to his tone. "Just 'cause I talked to the student council doesn't mean I'm gonna have a tea party with your buddy Ryan."

"A tea party," Sam echoed. "As if all they do in England is drink tea. What is it, really, that you don't like about Ryan?"

"He's just plain fussy," Jake said.

"What does he do that's fussy?" Sam demanded.

"I'm not tellin' you who to be friends with," Jake maintained, but his tone said someone should.

"No really, what is it?" Sam insisted. "His accent? The fact that he rides with an English saddle?"

"Yeah, and the way he dresses." Jake slowed the truck as they drove past the pastures that flanked both sides of the driveway.

"It's not like you to judge people because of the way they just are." Sam paused. When Jake looked uncomfortable, she pressed her advantage. "Really, I'm kind of disappointed."

"Good," Jake said gruffly as he pulled the van to a stop near the Slocums' arena. "Then you won't mind if I sit way off somewhere and don't talk to anyone. Me bein' such a disappointment, and all, I'd hate to embarrass you."

There was too much of an audience present for Sam to grab Jake's ears and rap his head against the driver's side door, so she only muttered, "You make me crazy."

"Mission accomplished," Jake replied, his smile white against his dark face. Then he nodded toward Ryan and Katie Sterling, both standing nearby, and gave Sam's shoulder a push. "See ya around, Brat."

Working alone, Sam unloaded Tinkerbell. He pranced down the ramp and surveyed Gold Dust Ranch. His ears flicked from the pony pasture to the cattle that looked like Oreos. He nickered at Hotspot, Linc Slocum's blue-blooded Appaloosa mare. Finally, he considered the people.

Ryan was already looking at him with appreciation.

"What a fine-looking fellow," Ryan greeted Tinkerbell, then added, "Hi, Samantha."

The gelding whuffled his lips over Ryan's coffee-brown hair before lipping his burgundy sweater.

Ryan allowed the inspection, then laughed. "Oh, we'll get along well. I'm sure of it."

"Hi, Sam." Katie Sterling wore an ivory-colored duster slung over her riding clothes. Though her outfit was practical and weatherproof, she managed to look like a fashion model. "We met before, when Rachel was looking for her last mount."

"Of course," Sam said, but when Katie met her eyes, Sam could tell they were both remembering their amazement when Rachel had bought a horse without even riding it. Appearance, not ability, had been Rachel's main concern.

Ryan had the tack ready. He'd extended the cinch and headstall on some existing gear and Tinkerbell protested neither. The English saddle was dwarfed by the gelding's mammoth stature, but Sam knew a Western saddle wouldn't look much different. Plus, it would be a disaster to use while jumping.

Sam saw no sign of the head-shyness Mr. Fairchild had mentioned. Tinkerbell mouthed the snaffle bit as if he hadn't worn one for a while, but that was all. Once he was tacked up, Tinkerbell watched Ryan with great interest.

"He looks sound," Ryan said as he pulled on a helmet. "Let's see how he goes."

The roofed arena had deep, soft footing from one end to the other. A few jumps were in place. Some painted rails, probably used for other jumps, were scattered around the middle of the arena.

Smooth and skillful, Ryan mounted, then took Tinkerbell around the arena.

Sam couldn't believe Tinkerbell's grace. He flowed through a walk, trot, and canter as if he'd been awaiting this for days. It was easy to forget the gelding's size.

Ryan's smile said he was just as amazed. When he brought the horse back to the side of the arena where Sam stood with Katie, his voice was filled with pleasure.

"His action is smooth. He responds to the lightest rein and he's very interested in the jumps."

Sam almost applauded. She'd been right. Tinkerbell was no throwaway horse.

"They were going to sell him for dog food," Sam blurted to Katie. "Can you believe it?"

"And you talked them out of it? When he could have been sold for hundreds of dollars?" Katie paused as Sam nodded. "You must be some talker."

"Not really," Sam said. "In fact, I'm—well, sort of afraid of, you know . . ."

As her voice trailed off, Sam wondered why she'd nearly confessed her fear of public speaking to Katie, when she'd only hinted at it to her friends and family.

"Don't be so humble," Katie said, with a half smile.

"No, really," Sam insisted.

Katie shook her head. "I've been working at the stable for years, renting stalls, selling horses, you name it. And I'll tell you, when you can get people to part with money, you're good."

For a minute, Sam was bewildered. She had convinced Mr. Fairchild they could earn a profit on Tinkerbell. But that was different.

"He works beautifully," Katie said.

Sam looked back at the arena, chagrined that she'd let her attention wander from Tinkerbell.

Hands and legs quiet, Ryan walked Tinkerbell toward the poles on the ground. His bucket-sized hooves just fit between them. Next, Ryan asked Tinkerbell to reverse direction and took the gelding back through the rails at a trot and finally a canter.

Where was Jake? Sam looked over her shoulder. He had to see this. She craned her neck to look back toward the cattle truck, but he was nowhere in sight.

Ryan's admiring chuckle carried from the center of the arena, as Tinkerbell tried to jump a row of rails instead of stepping between them.

"Patience," Ryan told the horse, and Tinkerbell's ears flicked back to listen.

"This ought to be fun," Katie said, as Ryan positioned the horse facing a small cross-rail fence.

It couldn't be more than a foot off the ground, so Sam didn't really see how it could be much of a test, but then she watched the gelding's reaction to it.

The jump was some distance off and Ryan gave Tinkerbell plenty of time to study it. The horse shifted in eagerness. Then Ryan must have given a signal, because Tinkerbell's dark ears flicked forward and his muscular front quarters tensed.

Sam held her breath as Tinkerbell skipped forward and popped over the fence. Ryan circled the arena and took Tinkerbell over the jump from the other direction, and then over a two-rail fence, which looked about three feet high.

"Oh, yes," Katie Sterling said under her breath.

When Ryan brought Tinkerbell back to Sam and Katie, he was grinning and shaking his head.

"He's a natural, isn't he?" Sam asked.

"On the contrary," Ryan said, dismounting. "Someone has worked with this horse. This is old hat to him. A green jumper will jump wide—leaving the ground early and landing well past the fence. This one," he gave Tinkerbell a pat, "is tidy as a cat. He saves his energy for moving his rather generous body around, and keeps his jumps neat."

Katie Sterling seemed to be waiting for something more. Her brows were arched as if she had a question.

Ryan glanced back down the arena, then looked back at Katie. "He could go much, much higher."

Katie's hands were fisted as she said, "I can't even ask if he's for sale, because I don't need him, but— wow."

"Actually, he might already be sold," Sam said. "Mr. Martinez is interested."

"Really?" Katie asked, an amused smile on her

lips. "I've seen his pasture fence. What's going to keep this big boy home if he decides he wants to go visiting?"

"He already did," Sam admitted.

"Ha!" Katie clapped her hands and looked back at Tinkerbell. "As soon as I can think of a way to justify buying him to my dad, I'll be making an offer."

Yes, Sam thought. Tinkerbell had two prospective homes. Maybe he'd be all right.

Suddenly, Ryan offered Sam the reins.

"Won't you take a turn now?" he asked.

She took a deep breath. Half of her wanted to give it a try. There couldn't be a safer place than right here in this arena, but what if she fell off? It wasn't like she'd never done that before, but she didn't want Ryan and Katie as witnesses.

And what if Rachel showed up? She lived only a few steps away, and though horses bored her, tormenting Sam might make it worth the walk from her mansion to the arena.

"You know, I'd like to," Sam said. "But Jake has to get back, and he drove us here." She looked around quickly for Jake. It would be just like him to tell her to go ahead.

"I understand." Ryan sounded disappointed, and his serious expression said he'd seen right through her refusal. He knew she was afraid to ride Tinkerbell.

All at once, Sam realized she didn't need Jake to

tell her to go ahead. She wanted to ride Tinkerbell. He could be sold tomorrow, and then she would have missed her chance. And if she fell—oh well, it wouldn't be the first time.

"I'll do it," Sam said. "But don't laugh. I've never been on a horse taller than sixteen hands."

"Great!" Ryan clapped her on the shoulder and set to work lengthening the stirrup leathers. "That's as long as they go."

The stirrups on the English saddle looked almost delicate. The bare little bars of metal were so different from the leather-wrapped ones on a Western saddle. Besides, these were higher than her eye level. How could she ever get her boot up there?

"I don't think that's going to do it," Sam said.

"I'll give you a leg up," Ryan said. He moved to stand next to Tinkerbell's neck and faced Sam.

Sam gazed up. "That's what you think," she muttered.

Fingers reaching, she snagged the reins, but barely. She should have a firm grip on them before she vaulted into the saddle. Otherwise, if Tinkerbell took off during her awkward mount, she wouldn't be going with him.

"You can do it," Katie encouraged. "You've got the reins, so just face the horse's shoulder, put your hand on his neck, or"—she laughed—"as high as you can reach. Then, you should put your other hand on the pommel. . . ."

"Just give me your left leg," Ryan said quietly as Katie continued her instructions.

With his own left leg bent and his hands cupped, Ryan boosted Sam as she sprang toward the saddle and suddenly, she was up!

The view from Tinkerbell's back was amazing. She looked down on Ryan's chocolate hair as if she'd climbed up into stadium bleachers, but she didn't feel the least bit unsteady.

"Don't look down," Katie joked. "Isn't that what they tell tightrope walkers?"

Sam laughed and patted Tinkerbell's satiny neck as Ryan adjusted the stirrups once more. She took up reins that were different from her Western reins. Instead of being split into two slick leather straps, the part she held was braided and buckled together. At least if she dropped them they wouldn't end up under Tink's hooves.

She settled into the small saddle as well as she could. Tinkerbell's back was so broad, her thigh muscles pulled, then complained, as she found her stirrups.

"Ready, boy?"

Tinkerbell's ears pricked forward and he gathered himself to step out.

"Now it's up to you," Ryan said. He swung one arm toward the arena, in invitation.

The draft horse was easy to ride. Sam smiled as she moved from a walk into a trot. Even at this bouncy gait, one thing was sure: she wasn't going to fall off, unless she really tried.

When they moved into a lope, or a canter, as Ryan called it, Sam imagined she heard the smooth, rhythmic music of a waltz. Tinkerbell rocked so gently and gracefully, Sam realized this was why circus bareback riders in tights and tutus performed on the backs of Percherons.

Tinkerbell's giant head bobbed as if he were keeping time. It was wonderful and fun.

When she finally drew him to a stop, Sam realized her legs weren't the only part of her that was strained from the ride. Her cheeks hurt from smiling.

She managed to dismount without her knees buckling.

As Ryan loosened Tinkerbell's girth and stripped off the English saddle, he lifted it in Sam's direction.

"Now that you know what an amazingly easy horse he is to ride, won't you take the tack along with you?"

"I guess I could borrow it," Sam said. "Thanks."

Sam was about to say more when Jake finally materialized.

"I'll take him, if you're going to carry that stuff," Jake said. He snagged the lead rope from Sam's hand.

"Thanks. But Jake, did you see him? 'Bye, Ryan," Sam said, waving as they headed for the truck. "Really, did you? The way he took those jumps and let me canter him around. Tink's an amazing horse. I need to wear different pants if I'm going to ride him with an English saddle, though."

Jake glanced back. Sam followed his eyes and noticed Ryan was still watching.

"All I can see you need is a mounting block," Jake said. "A rider oughta be able to put herself in the saddle."

Sam felt embarrassed and confused. Anyone would have trouble mounting Tinkerbell. Even Jake.

"Hey," she said. "I wasn't that bad."

She realized she would have had her hands perched on her hips if they hadn't been full of tack.

Jake's solemn expression vanished and he laughed.

"Settle down, Brat. You're scarin' the livestock," he said, though Tinkerbell looked happy and lulled by his time in the arena. "I'm just in a lousy mood 'cause I'm fixin' to crawl under the house when I get home."

"All right," Sam said with a satisfied nod.

"Now get in the truck and tighten your seat belt, 'cause we're gonna get on outta here, pronto."

Chapter Fourteen

Snow was swirling around the truck by the time they reached War Drum Flats. Jake turned on the truck's windshield wipers, but he didn't look a bit concerned. A kid who lived in northern Nevada learned to drive in snow or stayed home.

They drove in silence until Jake unexpectedly spoke up.

"That place could use some organization," he said. "I walked around a little and there's a barn full of empty stalls and tons of hay. Literally."

"I bet I know why," Sam said. "Remember that mustang baiting thing Linc got in trouble for?"

"Sure," Jake said.

Linc Slocum's grandiose plan for a resort called

Home on the Range had led him to feed wild horses at the roadside. He'd hoped when his investors came to visit, they'd see the mustangs as authentic Western atmosphere. Luckily, the BLM had cited and penalized him before any horses were struck by cars.

Though Jake didn't gloat, Sam could tell he felt the same way she did. Linc Slocum didn't get in trouble for every sneaky thing he did, but at least that time he'd been caught.

Getting caught. The words shouldn't remind her of her community service project, but they did.

"That wasn't just curiosity, was it? Earlier, when you asked about presenting your community service project to the student council."

"Are you psychic or something?" Sam demanded. "You read my mind way too often."

"It's not hard, when you're chewing on your bottom lip and frowning."

"No, it's not just curiosity. I'm scared to do that presentation." Sam felt resentment building. She hated admitting her fear. "Are you satisfied?"

"I'm gonna ignore your sarcasm. It took more guts to climb up on Tinkerbell than it will to do that presentation."

"No way," Sam said.

"There's not that much to it," Jake explained. "It's not dangerous. I mean, what's the worst thing that could happen? You forget what you're supposed to say? Big deal. So, bring notes. And they might not even notice if you get off track. Your audience isn't exactly brilliant."

"Jake! That's not nice," Sam scolded, but she had to admit he was making her feel more confident.

"Might not be nice, but it's accurate. You know Rachel and Daisy." Jake leaned a little closer to the windshield as the storm intensified. "All you need to do is make three good points. Then ask for what you want and sit down."

Jake could be right, but she still had to come up with a dynamite project.

Sam stared out at the snowflakes. They whirled like frenzied white gnats, reminding her of the Phantom, shaking his mane free of snow. Reminding her of the hungry horses. Reminding her . . .

"I've got it!" Sam shouted.

Jake grunted and gave her a sidelong glance.

"This is perfect! Oh my gosh, why didn't I think of this before? This will work. I know it will. Jake, I am so brilliant!" Sam folded her hands with a heavy, satisfied sigh. "Valentine's Day is just a week off."

"Yeah, so what?" Jake asked. "You're makin' me nervous, Brat."

"So, it'll be perfect timing. And your friend Darrell—I know just how he'll fit in."

"Okay, I'm not nervous anymore. Now I'm frightened."

Sam knew she was babbling, but her mind had just conjured up a plan. If Jen and Jake thought she could do it, maybe she could.

The Have a Heart project, she'd call it. People would donate money to feed the wild horses. It would be perfect, because it would keep the horses from starving *and* from sharing the cattle's fodder. And since Darrell's community service project was recycling tires, she'd bet he could get her a bunch to use as feeding rings for the horses.

"And Linc Slocum has tons of hay and Rachel needs this project as much as I do!" Sam crowed.

The truck slowed as Jake's foot hesitated on the gas pedal. He frowned, then asked, "Like, for a Valentine's Day hayride or something?"

"Of course not, Jake. Be quiet a minute and let me think."

He obeyed, although Sam thought he might have grumbled something a few minutes before they reached home.

Jake stopped the truck. When Sam started to get out, he reached across her and locked the door.

"What?" she asked.

"Tell me what's goin' on before I turn you loose on the world."

So, Sam rewound her spinning thoughts and explained. It sounded even better out loud, and apparently Jake agreed, because he wrote down Darrell's phone number so that she could call him right away.

"It could work," Jake admitted as they unloaded Tinkerbell.

"I know," Sam said, dreamily.

Still walking in a cloud of ideas thicker than the falling snow, she led Tinkerbell away from the cattle truck.

"Yeah, you're welcome!" Jake shouted after her. "Don't mention it! No problem! Just call on me for chauffeur services any day! It's what I live for!"

"Okay," Sam said, then she waved and kept walking toward the barn.

This time, Ace got him.

Because Sam was preoccupied, she ignored Tinkerbell's nervous sidestepping and crowding as they came into the barn. Ace flashed his teeth and raked them down Tinkerbell's neck.

"No!" Sam held tight to the lead rope as Tinkerbell shied. "I'm sorry, boy."

The attack was short-lived, but loud. Ace made all the noise, neighing and kicking his wooden stall.

Tinkerbell didn't bolt. He walked beside her into his stall and stood shaking. His lips moved in questioning, worried movements. His glossy brown neck wrinkled as it curved to look back at Ace.

Standing on tiptoe, Sam examined the bite. Ace's teeth hadn't broken the skin. Thank goodness. Tinkerbell's feelings were hurt more than his hide.

She talked to him, telling him he was a good horse, a pretty horse. She told him how proud she'd been when Ryan was riding him.

"And you were so good to me," Sam told him. "I was perched up there like a decoration, and you could have made me look real silly. But you didn't."

When Tinkerbell tired of her crooning and began searching his bedding for something to eat, Sam left, bolting the stall door behind her.

Ace was still staring. Not at her, either. He held his head high, glaring past her toward Tinkerbell's stall.

"What is your problem?" she shouted at Ace.

Her horse tossed his head in mock fear. He backed away, eyes rolling, as if she'd turned into a monster.

"You've had plenty of other horses to be jealous over. Popcorn, Sunny, Queen. What is it about him that makes you act crazy?"

Ace turned his tail to her. She guessed that was one way of saying he'd heard enough. The barn was cold. Snow blew through the gaps between boards in the old part of the barn and the timbers creaked. Sam rubbed her palms up and down the arms of her jacket and took a shuddering breath. She was yelling at Ace, but this was her fault. Every horseman knew it was dangerous to let your attention wander. She was just lucky her carelessness hadn't caused Tinkerbell to suffer more.

"What was all the commotion about?" Gram asked when Sam got to the house.

Sam shook the snow from her jacket before

hanging it, then told the truth. She waited for a lecture, but Gram had something else on her mind.

"Like I said last night, seems all the animals are crazy this week. There was that hubbub Thursday with the horses running around as if the sky was falling. The chickens are acting nutty, too. 'Course, they are not the cleverest of animals," Gram mused. "But when I drove in from church a little bit ago, Blaze was digging in my garden!"

"There's nothing growing this time of year, is there?"

"No honey, there's not, but I doubt Blaze knows that." She shook her head. "He's just not a digging dog. That makes his behavior downright unusual."

Sam sat still for a minute and realized she hadn't heard any footsteps on the stairs or on the floor overhead. "Where are Dad and Brynna?" she asked.

"They went into Darton to a movie," Gram said in a wondering tone. "I can't think when Wyatt last did that. Probably when you were little."

Sam felt a small twinge of jealousy. They could have waited for her. On the other hand, if they had, she wouldn't have the time to get started on her Have a Heart project and she was excited to begin.

Over a lunch of grilled peanut butter and honey sandwiches, she and Gram made lists of what she'd have to do to get things rolling before Valentine's Day.

"I'll get everything in place. Then I'll call Rachel," Sam said.

"That's up to you, dear," Gram said. "I've never been able to figure that girl out."

Don't try too hard, Sam thought. Beneath that cold, selfish exterior is a colder, even more selfish heart.

But maybe this time, since her semester grade was at stake, Rachel could work with her.

"You know what might appeal to her?" Gram asked, pointing her finger at Sam. "Do you know Lynn Cooper?"

"The television reporter?"

"Exactly. Brynna was talking about her just the other day. She's worked with Brynna on a couple stories about wild horses. Maybe she'd be interested in covering your Have a Heart idea."

"And Rachel would love to be on television!"

Sam hurried to look up the phone number for KVDV television. Before she lost her nerve, she dialed. Since it was Sunday, Lynn Cooper probably wouldn't even be in. It would be easy to leave a message.

Dialing, Sam smiled to herself. After this, she could honestly tell Rachel she'd been in touch with the media.

The reporter was in, after all.

"Lynn Cooper," said a deep, pleasant voice.

"Oh! My name is Samantha Forster," she began, and then stopped.

"Yes?"

"I guess I didn't expect you to answer," she admitted.

"I'm the Sunday anchor." The reporter sounded as if she were smiling. "What can I do for you?"

Sam explained her idea. Each time her voice trailed off, Gram pushed their list a little closer and Sam kept going.

"It sounds like my kind of story. Give me the date again."

"Well, I don't have one yet," Sam said. "But I can call you back."

"Do," the reporter said. "No guarantees, though. It will depend on whether it's a heavy news day or not."

"Okay, thank you," Sam said.

Didn't starving horses qualify as "heavy"? Maybe the reporter was giving her a polite brush-off.

"Breaking news—like a fire or an announcement from the governor's office—gets covered first," Lynn Cooper explained. "If you can't reach me in the office, here's my cell phone number." Sam wrote as the reporter recited. "But don't worry if you can't get me on it. There are black holes in cellular service throughout northern Nevada. Especially out near the Calico range. Samantha, I'd like to do the story. Wild horses coming down from the snowy mountains? If nothing else, the footage would be great. Keep in touch."

By three o'clock, Sam had made two more important phone calls. Things were going great.

"That would expand my recycling program,"

Darrell said after Sam explained. "You see, right now, auto shops and truck stops have to pay to have tires hauled away. If I can recycle them for free, it makes everyone happy.

"Yeah," he went on. "There's a truck stop out in Mineral with gigantic truck tires. They'll make bigger feeding rings, so more horses can gather around."

"Thanks, Darrell." Sam hurried to get off the phone. A thoughtful tone had crept into Darrell's voice and she didn't know what might come next.

"I'll get you all the tires you want," Darrell said. "Under one condition."

"What?" Sam asked carefully.

"I want to be in on the delivery," he said.

Sam thought a minute, turning the words this way and that, but she didn't understand what Darrell meant. "Huh?" she asked.

"Here's how we'll do it. I'll get a bunch of tires out to your place and then we'll hitch them up, one right after the other behind the big new horse of yours—"

"How do you know about Tinkerbell? I've only had him a few days."

"Darlin', I know everything!" Darrell laughed.

Darlin'?

"Darrell, maybe this is a mistake," she began in a cautioning tone.

"Consider it a sleigh ride, sorta. Let me get a ride in one of the tires on the way out and I'll get Jake to follow us with a truck fulla hay. If there are three of us setting things up, it'll go a lot faster. What do you say?"

Sam couldn't see any flaws in the plan. She'd get a chance to ride Tinkerbell at a slow, sedate pace. She'd have a couple extra sets of hands and, best of all, Darrell would be the one asking Jake for the favor this time. She said yes.

Next, she called Callie, a friend who'd adopted a wild horse from the Phantom's herd. Queen, a beautiful red dun, had been the Phantom's lead mare, but she'd been taken off the range with a badly cracked hoof. Queen and Callie had bonded right away and even though Callie was living on her own while she attended beauty college, she'd already managed to train the mare to lead.

When Callie heard Sam's plan to help Queen's "family," she agreed to help and made a fund-raising suggestion of her own. "On Tuesday, my classes are over early. I could come on campus at Darton High during lunch hour and give temporary henna heart tattoos to any student who donates money to the Have a Heart project."

"You always have good money ideas," Sam said.

"That comes with paying your own bills," Callie said. "And even though you're getting the first load of hay from the Slocums, what if the storms go on through spring? Hay will go up in price just when you need more of it."

It seemed like each piece of the project had fallen

into place. Except the most important one. Now, she had to call Rachel and get the hay.

"It's time," she told Gram.

"Go get 'em, girl," Gram encouraged her. "It will work. Rachel loves to primp and show off. She won't be able to resist the little heart tattoos and TV coverage."

Sam's fingers were still crossed when Rachel answered the phone.

Sam started talking. Fast. None of this would work without the Slocums' hay.

"Rachel, hi. This is Sam Forster. I'm sorry about our little run-in Friday, but I think I have an idea for a community service project that will get us both out of trouble with Mrs. Santos."

Rachel was quiet for a minute, probably weighing her pride against her semester grade. "Go ahead," she said.

Emphasizing how much fun it would be and how excited Lynn Cooper was about shooting the hay drop for television, Sam explained.

"That's kind of cool," Rachel said. "I'm amazed you thought of it."

"Gee, thanks, Rachel," Sam said, gritting her teeth.

"What's my part?" Rachel said, sounding a little pouty.

"Besides getting the hay from your dad," Sam said, slipping the big request in as an aside, "I think you should do public relations. You know, get the word out at school?"

"I could do that," Rachel said. "The Valentine idea will make it fun. Maybe I should contact Lynn Cooper, again, just so she knows she'll be dealing with me."

"Great!" Sam said. "We'll talk about it more at school tomorrow, but one last thing."

"What?" Rachel asked.

Sam tried to sound casual. "Do you think you'd have time to present this before the student council?"

Say yes, say yes, say yes, Sam's brain chanted.

"I can't do that. I'm a member of the council, so I can't introduce a project."

"Can't you abstain from the vote or something?"

"Nope, but if you want, I could get Daisy to introduce it."

Rachel couldn't have done a better job of convincing her to do it herself. A lot was riding on this idea and Daisy would undoubtedly mess it up.

"No, I guess I can do it."

"Good. The next meeting's tomorrow at lunch, but I'll get you on the agenda."

Sam gasped. "I don't—you don't—I mean, I can wait."

"It's no big deal," Rachel said. "We add last-minute items all the time."

"Okay," Sam squeaked. While her head was spinning, Rachel kept talking.

"I said," Rachel raised her voice, "what about the hay part? When do we need it?"

Sam exhaled. "Have Jed Kenworthy bring it over on Wednesday."

"Okay," Rachel said. "And Sam?"

"Yes?"

"I have these little heart stencils for my fingernails. I think they'll set just the right tone for our project. I'd like to talk longer, but applying them could take a while."

As Rachel hung up, Sam took a deep breath and picked up the list she'd made with Gram.

"I'm going to make some more notes for tomorrow," Sam said.

"You'll do fine," Gram said. "Just relax and smile and tell them what's on your mind."

"I can do that," Sam said, but as she walked up the stairs to her room, she wasn't so sure. Going into the student council meeting tomorrow would be like striding into a lion's den. And lions could smell fear.

Chapter Fifteen

Sam carried a folder full of notes and some brochures on wild horses that Brynna had given her. Her mental notes included hints on the ranchers' perspective from Dad. As she walked into Darton High's conference room for the lunchtime meeting of the student council, she decided she was as ready as she'd ever be.

Inside, she saw one familiar face. The council members, mostly juniors and seniors, were seated at a long conference table. Quinn Ely, one of Jake's brothers, lounged with his chair tipped on its back legs, eating a sandwich. With his black hair cut porcupine short and his long, lanky body, he was Jake's opposite except for his high cheekbones and bronze skin.

"Hey, Sam," Quinn called. His greeting made every eye rivet on her as she found a chair in the back of the room and slipped into it.

So much for being unobtrusive.

Quinn gave a wink, reminding her how he'd helped her pull a practical joke on Jake just a couple weeks ago. Quinn was definitely an individual, so how did he manage to fit in with all the popular kids on student council?

Maybe this would be different than she'd thought.

Twelve kids were seated by the time the meeting was called to order. Rachel still hadn't shown up and Sam couldn't believe she was disappointed. For what it was worth, she'd been counting on Rachel's support.

Just when she'd given up, Rachel and Daisy sauntered into the room.

"Sorry, sorry," Rachel apologized, but she smiled without an ounce of sincerity.

In passing, Rachel tousled the hair of a guy named Clark. Sam couldn't remember his last name, but he was the student body president and his blush was more vivid than Rachel's red silk blouse.

Rachel squeezed into a place across from Clark, took his copy of the agenda, and glanced at it.

"Where's Sam?" she asked coolly. "Samantha Forster's name belongs on the agenda. Clark, I told you this morning. Don't you remember?"

Sam's stomach lurched. Should she be disappointed that she'd done all this preparation for nothing? Or happy that she'd escaped?

Rachel whispered briefly with Clark. He might be student body president, captain of the chess club and rifle team, and widely regarded as one of the smartest kids on campus, but he was no match for Rachel's purring disapproval.

"Fine," he said in exasperation, and Sam thought his pressed green shirt looked more rumpled than it had two minutes ago. "We'll start with new business and she can go first."

Now? Sam wondered if her heart actually stopped. She'd counted on having at least a few minutes to watch and see how things were done.

"Samantha Forster?" Clark called. "Do you have a community service proposal?"

"Yes," Sam managed. She stood and drew a deep breath. "First I'm going to hand out some brochures, which will give you some background on our project."

She passed out the brochures, giving herself a minute to think.

So far, so good. Every student in the room was reading a brochure. Sam was feeling almost calm when the conference door opened once more to admit Mrs. Santos.

"Go right ahead, Sam," the principal said. She smiled, smoothed her skirt, and sat down, regarding

Sam with an attentive smile.

Just do it, Sam told herself.

And she did. Her voice trembled and she had to place her folder on the table because her hands were shaking too hard for her to read her notes, but people were still listening when she reached her conclusion.

"And so, because it's the humane thing to do, because local ranchers would welcome the help, and because it will show the community that Darton High students care about their environment, I hope the student council will approve the Have a Heart community service project."

It was over. Sam exhaled so loudly, several students laughed. And Rachel actually led the others in applause. Jen had told her to be ready for questions, but, as Sam glanced around the room, everyone looked satisfied.

Everyone except Clark. Instead of calling for a vote, the student body president cleared his throat.

"I don't know about this," he said, flapping his brochure in a pompous manner. Because he was, after all, president, the others turned to listen.

Oh, no. Sam felt dizzy. Why had she even tried? He was going to humiliate her and that would be a lot worse than working in the dump.

"Wouldn't you just be feeding nonnative species and pushing out native species like antelope and deer?"

All at once Sam remembered seeing a newspaper

photograph of Clark holding up the heavily antlered head of a dead white-tailed buck.

He was captain of the rifle team, so of course he was a hunter. Lots of hunters thought mustangs competed with game animals.

Give up now, ordered one cowardly portion of her brain. A braver voice in her mind asked, *If the Phantom could save you from starving, would he?*

She knew he would, so when the students turned toward her with a flurry of questions, she took a deep breath and answered. "As far as I know, cattle aren't native to the high desert and neither are sheep."

"But they're productive and we control their populations," Clark pointed out.

"That's right," Sam said. "And from what I've read, the mustangs used to have a controlled population, until people changed the environment by shooting predators for trophies."

Sam knew she'd either scored big or struck out. She held her breath, waiting to find out which it was.

"Oh yeah, Clark." Quinn laughed. "You've been schooled by the cowgirl!"

The other students laughed. It was rare to see anyone get the better of Clark. To his credit, the student body president shook his head with a half smile and called for a vote.

Two minutes later, the Have a Heart plan was approved.

Jen was waiting outside the office. Wind blew her

braids into her eyes, but Jen pushed them back so she could see Sam's face before they were near enough to talk.

Sam pumped her fist toward the snow-bellied clouds.

"You did it!" Jen crowed.

"I did," Sam said, amazed. She gave Jen a quick description of what had happened, then shook her head. "After I quit using my notes, it was almost easy."

"Passion," Jen said, solemnly.

"What?"

"Wild horses are your passion. So, when Clark forced you to defend them, you did it. Passionately."

"If you say so," Sam replied, raising her voice over the bell that signaled the end of the lunch period. "But right now, I care passionately about getting to Journalism, so Mr. Blair doesn't flunk me."

Good news was followed by better news.

After school, Gram had just handed Sam a brand-new set of clingy CoolMax long underwear to replace her bulky old knit top and leggings—"to keep you warm during the hay drop"—when Brynna called to say she'd talked with Lynn Cooper, the TV reporter.

"I assured her that, even though your project isn't BLM-sanctioned, you weren't some flaky kid. I told her you cared about the wild horses and definitely would make this project work."

Sam had just hung up the phone when Dad came in and offered the use of the hay truck, before she could ask.

"Wow, thanks," Sam said.

"That's if Jake drives," Dad cautioned.

"Of course," she said. "He already agreed to do it. Things are going so well, it's almost scary."

"Now, why would you say a thing like that?" Gram asked. "Just when I was about to make brownies, too."

"Not that scary," Sam said quickly. "You can still make brownies."

"I planned to," Gram said. "And with everything going on, don't forget to keep an eye on Cougar."

Sam glanced into a corner of the kitchen where Cougar was dancing on his hind legs, batting at the strings of an apron Gram had hung on a hook.

"He looks innocent now," Gram said, "But twice today, I've had to bend myself double to grab him before he could slip outside."

"He wants to go see Tinkerbell," Sam explained.

"That's very sweet," Gram said, "but it's dangerous outside for a kitten that small. Coyotes, snow, even a misplaced hoof . . ." Gram shook her head. "He's a delicate little thing."

After dinner, Jen called with the only bit of bad news Sam had had so far.

"You're doing the hay drop on Wednesday, aren't you?" Jen asked. "I can't go."

"Oh no, why?" Sam thought fast. Before Jen could answer, though, she knew she couldn't delay the hay drop. The horses were hungry.

"Last week I agreed to baby-sit Hotspot while my parents go into Reno for a Palomino Breeders Association meeting. They plan to leave as soon as I get home from school."

"It's cool that they're planning to rebuild the Kenworthy palomino idea," Sam said. Years ago, Jen's parents had begun breeding a spectacular line of palominos called Fire and Ice for their fiery gold coats and pure white manes. With the loss of several horses, the program had stalled out, but only temporarily.

"I know," Jen agreed, "so I can't really complain. Besides that, Hotspot could foal any time and there's no way they'd leave her in the care of Linc and Rachel."

Sam shuddered. "No way. But what about Ryan?"

"What about him?" Jen asked, but Sam could hear the smile in her voice.

"Oh, I see, you two are going to be watching Hotspot *together*."

"That could happen," Jen said. "So while I'm sorry I won't be able to go with you on Wednesday—"

"You're not exactly heartbroken," Sam finished for her, and Jen's giggles were all the agreement Sam needed.

Just then, she noticed Dad standing in the doorway as if he had something to say. "Gotta go, Jen. See you tomorrow."

With her hand still on the phone, Sam waited for Dad to speak. When he didn't, she asked, "What did I do?"

Dad smiled. "Nothing wrong, hon. You're doing real well, and since Mrs. Santos wants you kids to accomplish these projects on your own, I'll try my best not to interfere."

"Thanks, Dad," Sam said, although the promise made her a little uneasy.

"Just be careful, Sam." Dad's eyes clouded with a familiar worried expression. "You know what I think about every time you do something risky."

"The accident." Sam felt her confidence wobble just a little.

"That's right, but so far you've used pretty good judgment, so I'm going to keep trusting you." Dad kissed her on the cheek before he went outside to check the livestock for the night.

Sam had turned to leave when his voice called her back.

"Sam, honey, just don't be too proud to call it off, if things start going wrong."

By the end of school the next day, money had poured in for the Have a Heart project. Not only were the henna heart tattoos selling like crazy, a

Western wear store had called to donate the cost of a ton of hay.

When Sam arrived home, she found Linc Slocum's hay and six huge truck tires piled just outside the half-completed new bunkhouse. It was lucky construction had been stalled by the snowy weather, Sam thought, because the hay bales and tires formed a barricade five feet tall.

Working with Pepper and Ross, Sam helped cover the hay with tarps. The snow kept piling up and more was expected tonight. It was a good thing only twenty-four hours remained until she, Jake, and Darrell dragged the hay out to the horses' winter range. "Saw that mustang herd just across the river today," Pepper said as they cinched down the ropes binding the tarps.

"What were they doing?" Sam asked.

"Pawing at the snow on the cattle's summer range," he said disapprovingly. "If they keep that up . . ."

"Every minute we wait, they're getting hungrier," Sam said. "I wish we could go right now."

"Well, you can't," Pepper said. "But you can sure help me dump the snow that's melted inside those tires. If you leave 'em that way, they'll be frozen by morning and even your monster horse won't be able to pull them."

Sam was helping Gram make dinner when Brynna came home from work. Sam was about to thank her again for talking with Lynn Cooper, but she stopped.

Brynna stood in the middle of the kitchen, frowning. The snow on her coat had begun dripping when she finally spoke.

"We've got a colt in off the range. A yearling," she said. Her freckles stood out like sand on her pale cheeks. "Don't ask me if he's from the Phantom's herd, Sam, because I don't know. He's dark bay and he's hypothermic. That's what I do know. We trailered him out to Mrs. Allen over at the Blind Faith Mustang Sanctuary, and Dr. Scott met us there. He's in good hands, but I don't know if he'll live."

Brynna took a shuddering breath before she explained that a snowmobile had seen three horses trapped in a snow yard. They'd trampled down an area, looking for food, and inadvertently walled themselves in. All three of them were trapped there.

In dismay, Brynna looked up at Gram.

"Sakes, I've heard of deer doing that," Gram said. "But never horses."

Brynna shook her head and stared at the kitchen window. It was black. It held no answers, only reflected her image.

"What happened to the yearling?" Sam asked.

"The guy rammed his snowmobile against the ice fence—"

"Oh my gosh!" Sam gasped. Wild horses were terrified by the flutter of a human hand. How would they have reacted to a roaring machine?

"He was trying to help." Brynna sounded defeated. "And two of them did get out. They ran, but the yearling collapsed."

"Can you call—" Sam began.

"I won't check until tomorrow," Brynna said. "They'll have their hands full tonight, no matter what happens."

After dinner, Sam tried to do homework, but she couldn't concentrate. She tried to sleep, but her eyes stared at the ceiling until she saw nothing but a frenzy of dots. Were the three horses from the Phantom's herd? Would the horses feed from tires once they were in place? And who would pay one thousand dollars for Tinkerbell?

The phone rang downstairs. Sam looked at the glowing numerals on her watch. It wasn't that late, but Jen knew not to call after nine. Sam sighed. What else could go wrong?

Shut up, she told her mind. *You don't want to know.*

"Sam?" Dad called. He didn't sound happy.

She padded down the stairs, dodging Cougar as she went.

Maybe it was Mr. Martinez. Maybe he'd changed his mind. But the voice she heard was Rachel's.

"Tell me nothing's wrong," Sam ordered.

"Nothing's wrong. Settle down, cowgirl," Rachel said, stiffly. "In fact, KVDV television definitely wants to shoot footage of you delivering the hay."

"Lynn Cooper called you?" Sam asked.

Sam's spirits lifted as if they had wings. Tinkerbell would look absolutely heroic marching through the snow, bringing food to his wild cousins.

"Actually, she was returning my call. And of course they want me to be there, because I am quite photogenic." Rachel paused. "Still, Lynn Cooper wouldn't promise me camera time. If you ask me, she's a little jealous."

Sam pictured the reporter's fresh, open face and blond hair that always looked stylishly windblown. Of course Rachel was wrong, but what was the point in contradicting her? Besides, Sam was thinking of other things.

Although Have a Heart didn't need television coverage to succeed, it would almost certainly help Tinkerbell.

Maybe Lynn Cooper would fall in love with Tink's sad Cinderella story and do a long feature segment on him. They could talk about his close call at the Mineral Auction yards and Ryan could show off the gelding's jumping skills. Best of all, someone might see Tinkerbell on television and make an offer to buy him.

". . . and my family does have a reputation for donating to worthy causes . . ."

Suddenly Sam realized what Rachel was saying. She didn't look forward to spending time with the rich girl, but it would only be fair. She was doing a good deed; she should get her face on the news.

"Rachel, of course you should come with us."

A sputtering laugh indicated to Sam that she was way off base.

"Freeze half to death and be photographed with a nose red from the cold?" Rachel asked. "You must be joking. If she can't come here, or at least to school to interview me, she's out of luck."

Shaking her head, Sam trudged back up to bed. At least she wouldn't have to spend tomorrow afternoon with Rachel. That was a blessing, because she knew Rachel would have complained about the wind, the cold, the flying bits of hay, and having to ride a horse out to the range, instead of sitting in the backseat of her cozy Mercedes.

For the second night in a row, Sam had a hard time falling asleep. Her mind was just too full. She thought of Hotspot's and Dark Sunshine's foals. She worried that all the activity of dragging the hay bales out to the range would make the mustangs scatter. And she worried just a little bit that she'd have trouble riding Tinkerbell all the way out to the foothills of the Calico Mountains.

At last she dozed, but her sleep wasn't peaceful. In one dream, she soared above toy-sized people, horses, and a whirlpool of vivid blue water. It spun around and around until she was hypnotized and fell toward its vortex.

Sam decided the dream was prophetic the next afternoon, when Rachel used the Journalism room telephone to call Lynn Cooper and discovered the reporter was out on a story.

I should have known, Sam thought. That dream meant all my hopes for a second rescue for Tinker are going down the drain.

"She left us a stupid message, though," Rachel said. "She said if she and the camera crew weren't at River Bend by three thirty, you should go ahead and they would catch up with you."

"Good," Sam said. "At least she's still planning on coming."

"I forgot," Rachel employed her British accent to sound mature and superior. "You never do see unkindness when it's coming right at you. She won't come. She's just trying to let you down easy."

By three forty-five that afternoon, Sam was beginning to wonder if Rachel had been right.

The film crew from KVDV still hadn't arrived. Sam hated to leave before it did, but she and the guys had to beat the storm.

Although they pretended to be having coffee and pie in the kitchen, Sam knew all three adults were eager for them to go.

Wrapped in a long, lined trench coat, Brynna came out on the front porch.

"We wouldn't be interfering if we told the reporter how to find you, would we?" Brynna pretended to sound casual, but she was the one who'd announced that weather reports said the roads might be impassable by evening.

"That'd be great," Sam said. "We're going to leave in a few minutes, anyway."

With Tinkerbell brushed and beautiful and the ranch truck belching black smoke out its tailpipe, they crossed the River Bend Bridge and waited on the wild side of the river.

Coming home on the bus, the storm hadn't looked threatening. Snow had wavered like a gauzy curtain between the La Charla River and the mountains.

Now, the mountains were invisible. Sam was glad to have Tinkerbell and the guys along. She'd been lost in a snowstorm once before and she'd hated it. Even her horse hadn't known which direction to go.

"Let's hit it," Jake said. "This weather is only gonna get worse."

Sam checked her watch. "Five minutes more," she told him.

Darrell was using the extra minutes to test the knots holding each tire to the next. He planned to ride in the second-to-the-last tire.

"This is gonna be great," he told Jake. "Riding in this one will give me lots of snap, and I won't get a face full of snow from that monster's feet.

"They're good and tight," Darrell said, turning to Sam.

Sam smiled. Darrell was taking his "sleigh" ride seriously. When she'd fretted that he might fall and get tangled in the ropes, Darrell had actually pulled out a wicked-looking pocketknife and brandished it.

"I can cut myself loose, darlin'. Don't worry your pretty head."

Sam looked down the highway once more. It was completely empty.

"I wish you guys had worn red," she grumbled. She fidgeted, though her red pullover fit snugly under her jacket. "Brynna says red looks good on television. Besides, this is a Valentine's Day fundraiser, you know."

Both guys ignored her.

"Why are you in such a rush? You have chains," Darrell pointed out to Jake.

"Yeah," he said, "and it's time to use 'em. I'm out of here."

Jake yanked open the ranch truck's door and climbed inside.

"Might as well," Sam said. She gave him a head start and then sent Tinkerbell after him. Clots of snow flew from Tinkerbell's hooves. His big body surged into the wind and Sam thought of rajahs on elephants. Perched on the draft horse's back, she had a bird's-eye view of everything around her.

Still, the hay truck drew away quickly, and soon it was out of sight.

"Dashing through the snow!" Darrell bellowed.

His voice sounded lonely floating over the barren range, but Sam didn't order him to stop the Christmas carol. Tinkerbell liked it, and as long as he was happy, he wouldn't notice the hundreds of pounds of truck tires sliding along behind him.

Sam pulled down her cowboy hat. It didn't match the English saddle, but it helped shade her eyes from the snowflakes fighting to clump on her eyelashes. She urged Tinkerbell into a jouncing trot and reined him in a weaving motion that made Darrell crow in delight.

"Hang on, Zanzibar," Sam whispered. Her secret name for the Phantom was safe while the wind whipped her words away.

The foothills were finally in sight when they caught up with Jake. He was standing beside the truck. Its hood was up. Jake's hands were on his hips as he peered inside.

"What happened?" Sam shouted through the wind.

"It's dead."

"Are you sure?" Sam asked. It was Dad's truck. "It can't be dead."

"Well, I'm no expert," Jake said, "but when an engine clatters like crazy, then pops like the Fourth of July, and stops, it's either dead, or needs to be put out of its misery."

Chapter Sixteen

𝒯here was no sense in complaining. Dad had said she should know when to quit, but this was not the time.

Together, they decided she and Darrell could continue out to the feeding site, position the tires, then she'd ride back to the truck, where Jake would have bound the hay into several large bundles and Tinkerbell could drag the hay to the tires.

It had to be two miles between the truck and the feeding site, and the mustangs might spook and run by the time they returned, but they really had no choice.

Tinkerbell trudged through the snow, head held so low that Sam was the first to spot the Phantom.

He stood on a high ridge, observing the strange parade of creatures trespassing on his territory.

"Perfect," Sam breathed.

The stallion was here, so his herd must be nearby. She glanced back over her shoulder and motioned for Darrell to look, but he was leaning back in a tire, eyes closed as if he were sunning on a beach.

Suddenly, Tinkerbell was rearing. Sam threw her weight forward, but Tinkerbell didn't feel it. Grabbing, she filled both hands with mane. At last, he lowered.

Had he smelled the wild horses?

No. He wasn't acting excited. Tinkerbell was afraid. He jumped, though there was nothing to jump over. He jerked each hoof up the minute he set it down, as if the ground jolted him with electricity.

Sam tightened her reins, but the gentle snaffle was nothing to Tinkerbell. If Jake were here — but he wasn't. She had to use her rider's instincts to figure out what was wrong with the horse and keep him from hurting her and Darrell.

"Yank it!" Darrell yelled, and Sam pulled the release rope holding the tires in place.

As she did, a wave of dizziness swept over her. Not from looking down. The white world around her blurred as if she were riding a runaway carousel. The snowy plain before her lurched. Her head reeled and she fought for balance. She tried to focus on the ridge, on something solid, but even that rocky outcropping wobbled before her eyes.

Crack! Like a shotgun blast, the noise cut across all other sounds, then spread into a roar. On the ridge, a kaleidoscope of crystals spun, erasing the Phantom. Where had he gone? A white cloud of snow blew up and out. Could it be an avalanche? Could it have swept the Phantom off the ridge?

"Earthquake!" Darrell shouted.

Sam reeled. In San Francisco the word made sense, but not here. Except that an earthquake could cause an avalanche, or cause a huge horse like Tinkerbell to stagger, as he was doing now.

Then Tinkerbell was running.

There was no stopping him. Sam clung to his neck instead of sawing at the reins. Her tugging might put him off balance. Instead, she fought to keep her boots on the thin metal bars of the English stirrups. She battled to find some rhythm in his headlong zigzag run, but he was running scared.

She lost her right stirrup. She couldn't breathe as she slid halfway down the gelding's barrel. Tinkerbell grunted with exertion, and Sam heaved herself back toward the saddle. Her grip on his mane helped, and finally she hauled herself up.

Sam was afraid to look back, afraid she'd bounce free of the saddle altogether, but she needed to see if Darrell was safe.

Tinkerbell vaulted over nothing. Was the ground still shaking? Was he fighting gravity, trying to stay above the earth he could no longer trust?

Sam snatched a quick glance over her shoulder, then buried her face in Tinkerbell's mane once more. She'd glimpsed the tires and Darrell and horses running before a tidal wave of snow. The Phantom was fleeter than any of them. He must have made it down the mountainside ahead of the avalanche.

"Please, please," Sam chanted. "Oh, please let him be safe."

She looked back one more time, and the stallion was there, just three horse lengths behind her. As she watched, his powerful shoulders thrust his forelegs farther, faster. In an instant, he was running beside her.

The stallion was huffing, breathing harder than she'd ever heard him. His nostrils were wide and red from exertion. His brown eyes rolled toward her, recognizing her, checking her, as he slowed to match Tinkerbell's pace.

At the stallion's snort, Tinkerbell glanced right. His hooves stuttered and for one awful second, Sam imagined going down beneath the draft horse. Then a sigh flowed through him, and Tinkerbell fell into step with the Phantom.

Tinkerbell still ignored the reins, but his run was steady.

Sam risked another glance back, to see if the Phantom's herd was following. As she did, the stallion veered away, toward the dark shapes way back there, which must be his herd. Sam couldn't say good-bye, couldn't wish he'd stay. Zanzibar had kept her safe in the only way he knew, ordering Tinkerbell to slow his headlong panic into a rhythmic gallop.

When the stallion left, Tinkerbell didn't follow. He was going to the only home he knew—River Bend.

Ahead, Jake's silhouette stood black against the snow. His arms windmilled, trying to stop Tinkerbell, but the big gelding saw him and ran left. Jake's shout was a puff of sound with no words.

They swept past Jake, the truck, more miles of snow, and galloped on.

By the time the ranch came into sight, Tinkerbell had settled into a solid, rideable gait. It gave Sam time to realize that all the animals' weird behavior made sense.

The horses had sensed something, even last week. So had the chickens and the cattle. She'd read about such phenomena after a minor quake in San Francisco. Some scientific labs were using mice to predict earthquakes and claimed they were every bit as accurate as technical instruments.

"Good boy," Sam crooned to Tinkerbell. His ears flicked back, but he kept running. He might have been going home alone.

Sam tried to convince herself everything would be fine. Sure, it would be embarrassing to arrive home on a runaway. But Tinkerbell was listening to her hands on the reins, now.

It would be extra work to go back out on the range to put the hay in the holders. It would be bad for Tinkerbell's future—not to mention humiliating— if TV cameras caught any part of this. But she was pretty sure Darrell and the mustangs were safe. The TV crew might even arrive in time to pick up Jake and Darrell. And if Jake was mad? Oh well, Jake had been angry before. He'd get over it.

Ahead, she saw the big green volunteer fire department truck bucking along the highway. Fire? In all this snow?

Sam's stomach dropped. Of course, the earthquake. When the earth pitched and twisted, pipes broke. Not just water pipes, but gas. Fires could flare, ignite houses and barns. Relief weakened her as the truck racketed on by, passing the River Bend bridge.

Maybe it was just a precaution. Maybe they were making the rounds, checking on all the far-flung neighbors. Maybe Dad was even with them.

Maybe, but that didn't keep her from imagining the destruction such a strong quake could cause at home. A new sense of urgency gripped her.

She gave Tinkerbell his head and as they crossed the bridge she realized something really was terribly wrong.

The roofline of the barn was different. And someone was screaming. Not someone, a horse. A horse was screaming endlessly.

Tinkerbell headed right for the sound, running past a strange truck with an antenna on top, past the ten-acre pasture where the saddle horses circled the fence line, past the ranch house, toward the ruined barn.

A random thought surfaced suddenly in her brain. The difference between a hero and everyone else, she'd read once, was that a hero ran toward danger. If that was true, Tinkerbell had been bred to be heroic.

Before they reached the barn, Dad stepped into Tinkerbell's path. The horse slowed and let him grab the reins near the bit.

"Dad!" Sam shouted, but a sigh shuddered through her chest, stopping her words as she slid into his arms.

It was good to get off Tinkerbell's plunging back, but this was a nightmare.

The old section of the barn had collapsed. For the first time, Sam could see its real structure. Like huge tic-tac-toe squares made by timbers, the barn walls had crashed to the right. The horses inside were trapped.

"It's Sweetheart," Sam gasped. She recognized the pinto's high-pitched neigh. "But what about Ace?" Sam stared into her father's face. "Dad? Did Ace get out? Dad?"

"Honey, they're both still inside," Dad said.

Sam pulled away from his arms and ran toward

the barn. If anything happened to Ace, her heart would break.

Dallas grabbed her before she'd run very far. "Stay back. We'll get them out, fast as we can."

Brynna and Gram came jogging from the house.

"The power's out, but everything's okay inside," Brynna shouted. "It's only the barn and the new bunkhouse." Brynna gestured vaguely. "The radio says to stay outside. There could be aftershocks or a second quake, an even stronger one."

"Thank God you're all right." Gram grabbed Sam and hugged her.

Pepper and Ross had been squatting near the barn. Now they approached Dad.

"It's gonna go," Ross said.

"If we're gonna get those horses out before they're crushed, we've got to try now," Pepper said.

Sam kept staring at the barn. Her mind tried to make sense of the building she'd known all her life. It was half gone.

"I've got an idea," Dad said finally. "The roof's sagging, but it hasn't caved in. We'll prop it up with lumber from the bunkhouse, chainsaw those two uprights," Dad said, pointing. "Pepper, you're following me, aren't you?"

"Yeah, boss," said the young red-haired cowboy. "I'm going to get a harness."

"You're gonna hitch this horse"—Dallas paused to point at Tinkerbell—"to the crosspiece and have him pull the section out? It's risky. It could bring it all down if the props don't hold."

"Got a better idea?" Dad asked.

Sam wouldn't let herself picture the tons of woods and hay collapsing. Almost anything would be better than a second quake.

There was silence while Dad, Brynna, Gram, and the cowboys looked at each other. They were a team. Everyone had a voice in the awful decision.

"Let's do it," Brynna said.

"He's got the heart for it," Gram seconded.

In moments, Tinkerbell was in position.

Dallas slapped the reins on Tinkerbell's back. He shifted from hoof to hoof, but he didn't move forward.

"What's wrong with him?" the old foreman shouted.

"He's scared," Sam said.

It was the first time she'd seen him nervous. Still lathered with sweat from his run, Tinkerbell's eyes rolled as the timbers groaned and creaked behind him.

He gave a quick, nervous nicker and an answer came from the ruined barn. Sam recognized the nicker and her heart leaped up.

"Ace!" Sam shouted. She looked at Gram. "It's Ace!"

"Shh, honey, I know. Keep still, though. If he's hurt, we don't want him struggling."

The picture Gram's words painted was awful. Fallen timbers could do terrible damage to Ace's delicate face and slender legs.

"Okay, we're gonna do this in one pull. If it works, we'll have an opening we can lead them through in about one minute. Let's go, Tinkerbell!" Dad grabbed the gelding's cheekpiece and strode forward.

In a single tug, the gelding wrenched the section free. It rattled loose. Tinkerbell had pulled so hard, the chunks of wood followed him halfway across the yard.

Dallas dropped the reins. Dad released his hold on the bridle. As one, the men darted to the barn and peered through the opening, while Gram stopped Tinkerbell.

It was then that Sam noticed the television camera and remembered the strange vehicle she'd noticed as she thundered by on the big draft horse.

Apparently it had been focused on Tinkerbell and the struggle to decide what to do. A blond woman waved, not as if she wanted Sam's attention, but just in recognition. It must be Lynn Cooper, but Sam couldn't return her wave. Nothing mattered except Ace.

Before she reached the barn, she saw Pepper duck into the opening.

"He's the smallest and most flexible," Brynna said of the young cowboy. "If anyone can get over that wreckage and get the horses out, it will be him."

Suddenly, Sam realized her teeth were chattering.

Of course the weather was cold and it was still snowing, but this frigid grip was inside her. She was so afraid.

There was a squeal and the sound of hooves clattering on wood. Sweetheart, blanketed in dirt-smeared purple, worked free of the barn. Trembling, she looked around, trying to make sense of her home. But when Pepper gave her a gentle smack on the rump, the old mare knew what to do.

Eyes rolled white, she trotted forward, then bucked, heels kicking at the sky before she bolted for the ten-acre pasture and her friends.

"One more," Dad said, clapping Pepper on the shoulder.

"And the kitten," Ross said.

"Cougar?" Sam gasped. She turned to Brynna, but her stepmother's arm was already around her shoulders.

"He slipped out just before the quake, looking for Tinkerbell, we think. I was running after him when it struck." Brynna glanced down and Sam saw dirt on the knees of her stepmother's BLM uniform. "But cats do well in earthquakes. I've heard it time and again."

A sudden rumble was followed by a creak like a giant hinge. An aftershock. But only the timber slanting on the right side of the opening swayed and fell. Something metal clanged and shifted, and then Sam saw his face.

Black forelock blown back by a gust of snowy wind, Ace emerged from the barn. The white star on his forehead shimmered in the harsh winter light. Twisting free of Pepper's grip, he scrambled clear of the fallen timbers and bolted toward Sam.

Sam cried out, but the sound she made had no words. Her arms circled Ace's neck and she cried into his dirty winter coat.

Vaguely, she heard a voice tell her to watch out, but all she felt was sudden warmth. Sniffing, she pulled her face away from Ace's neck and realized she was sandwiched between two horses. The other one was Tinkerbell.

This time, the two geldings didn't quarrel. They touched noses and uttered curious nickers.

"Just the same," Dad said, towing Sam from between the two animals. "I'd feel better if you stood over here. Besides, here comes one more."

Sam's eyes followed Dad's pointing finger.

Cougar sat on a board that bobbed like a teeter-totter. Covered with straw and sawdust, the kitten was a mess, but he was very interested in cleaning one front paw.

The power came back on in time for Gram to fix an early dinner of hot roast beef sandwiches, then hustle them to everyone clustered around the television for the KVDV newscast.

"Oh my gosh, we're the lead story!" Sam yelped,

as a picture of Cougar filled the television screen.

"Good things come in small packages," said the lilting voice of Lynn Cooper. "Or do they?" The camera pulled back to include Tinkerbell.

The close-up showed the horse head-on, muscles glinting with sweat as he strained against the harness and jerked down the section of the barn.

Against the taped cheers of the Forsters and their cowboys, the reporter's voice went on, identifying each member of the family as they pitched in.

When Jake and Darrell staggered in from the range, the camera caught their amazement at the sudden destruction, but Lynn Cooper's casual manner encouraged even Jake to talk. Darrell grinned into the camera as if he'd been born to it.

Picking hay from his hair, Darrell said, "It'll all be worth it if I get an A on my community service project." And then he winked at the camera.

The news segment proceeded to show local destruction. There was a lot of it. There'd been a grease fire in Clara's Diner, water damage to several stores in the Crane Crossing Mall in Darton, and damage reports were still coming in from homes and ranches around the state. Lynn Cooper promised Darton Valley residents that the late news would feature more information regarding Federal Disaster Relief funds and how high the earthquake had registered on the Richter scale.

The report closed with a view of the reporter

standing on the edge of the playa. Covered with snow, with the sun going down, it was the color of peach ice cream.

"It's been a tough day in Darton Valley," said the reporter as wisps of blond hair blew across her forehead and wind whooshed over her microphone. "And no one at our station would minimize it, but as I returned to the studio, I couldn't help but take heart." She smiled.

"We lost no lives in today's earthquake. Families pulled together to save their livestock and pets. And Darton High School's community service program pressed on as planned, feeding at least some of the West's wild horses. . . ."

The camera panned behind her to show the Phantom's herd gathered around the tires. Blue shadows showed in the drag marks where Tinkerbell, Sam, Darrell, and Jake had managed to put out the tires and hay.

As the camera rose toward blue Nevada skies, Sam was scooting closer to the TV screen when the phone began to ring.

Katie Sterling was calling to make an offer for Tinkerbell.

Then Mr. Martinez called, asking if Sam had heard from Katie.

"Please, if she makes you a decent offer, accept it," he said, "but under no circumstances should we let that magnificent horse return to the auction."

Sam was explaining all the excitement to Gram, when Jake and Darrell followed Dad out the door.

"Where are they going?" she asked, but Gram was handing her the phone again and, for some reason, she rolled her eyes.

"I see you managed to get on television," Rachel sneered. "How convenient that Lynn Cooper drove right past my house to get to your rundown ranch."

Sam almost choked on her laugh. "Rachel, we didn't plan the earthquake—"

But the telephone receiver slammed down and she was talking to herself until Katie Sterling called again.

"Okay, Sam, I've talked with my dad and I can go up to two thousand dollars. I know it isn't that much, but I can promise you we'll jump him, take good care of him, and you have visiting privileges."

"Sold!" Sam said. She felt giddy with relief, but she still craned her neck to look out the kitchen window at the sound of an engine roaring to life.

Dad's blue pickup truck was pulling away with the boys crammed into the front seat beside him.

"Where are they going?" Sam repeated, as soon as she'd hung up.

Brynna swept into the kitchen, jingling her car keys.

"They're going to check on the truck. You and I are going to check on the mustangs! Grace, do you want to go?"

"I've had quite enough excitement for one day," Gram said. "I think I'll take a long, hot shower and go to bed early."

As good as that sounded, going with Brynna sounded even better.

The snow clouds had cleared and although it was evening, the range was washed in an odd milky light. Brynna's white truck was almost silent compared to the ranch vehicles, but she and Sam didn't talk.

Sam thought of the avalanche and the Phantom's loud, huffing breath. He was wild. He was in better condition than any cow pony. He'd be fine.

"Sam," Brynna said, suddenly, "we're so proud of you."

"Thanks," Sam said, but her eyes were scanning the range.

"When you rescued Tinkerbell, you started a chain reaction of good deeds. I know it sounds sappy, but don't worry about the Phantom. More often than not, all those good deeds circle back to the one who started them."

Sam smiled at her stepmother.

Dusk had fallen and the inky blue sky showed silver pinpricks when they were still a mile from the feeding site.

"We probably won't see them," Brynna said. "They'd feel awfully exposed to predators out here, this late."

"You can turn around if you want to," Sam said,

yawning, but then she spotted the ridge where the Phantom had been earlier.

"Stop!" she yelled.

Brynna applied the brakes quickly, but quietly.

"I'm guessing you see him," Brynna said, handing Sam her binoculars.

"I think so," Sam whispered, though she knew the stallion couldn't hear her.

The avalanche had created a choppy white sea of snow down below, but up where the Phantom stood, Sam saw green.

She focused the binoculars. A bit of green grass beneath the stallion's hooves promised spring was coming.

The stallion lifted his head. Sam couldn't see his eyes, but his mane drifted like a wisp of cloud as if he was sniffing the air.

I'm here, Zanzibar, she told him silently. *I'm here.*

As if he heard, the stallion rose onto his hind legs and reared. His delicate white forelegs pawed in a blur, silhouetted against the darkening sky, reaching for the stars.

From

Phantom Stallion
✥ 10 ✥
RED FEATHER FILLY

"The Super Bowl of Horsemanship?" Jen read from a typed page.

"Yes, indeed," Mrs. Allen said proudly. "Right here in your own backyard."

"I don't think I've ever heard of it," Sam ventured. She didn't want to sound ignorant about something to do with horses, but she really hadn't.

"That's because I just created it," Mrs. Allen said. "And first prize is enough money to make your head spin."

That wouldn't take much, Sam thought. She'd love to buy a new saddle. The one she used looked just like what it was—a handed-down kid's saddle.

Sam scooted her chair so that she could read the typed page right-side-up.

Mrs. Allen leaned back and savored a butter cookie while Sam and Jen read silently.

The Super Bowl of Horsemanship required horse and rider to complete an "extreme" obstacle course like those used for training police horses. It would include loud noises, visual distractions, and surprises to test the horse's confidence in his rider. After a short quarter mile of chaos, the race would cover seven miles of rough terrain.

Sam smiled as she studied the course map. She could already see herself winning. She knew every foot of sagebrush and alkali flat that made up the course.

Leaving from Deerpath Ranch, the race headed straight across the range for La Charla River. Once through the river, the trail turned south. It passed right by River Bend, then turned east at the Gold Dust Ranch. There, the racecourse crossed the river again, before running across War Drum Flats and back to the finish line at Deerpath Ranch.

A thrill of excitement tickled up Sam's arms and legs. She wasn't the best rider around, but she and Jen rode that territory all the time. Familiarity had to count for something, didn't it?

So, why wasn't Jen hooting with joy?

When Mrs. Allen tapped the date printed on the sheet, Sam looked. It was only two weeks away, on the last weekend of spring break.

"Even though the race isn't too demanding, Dr. Scott thought vets should check each horse twice." Mrs. Allen held up two fingers. "Before the race and at the finish line. If the animals show the slightest sign of abuse, the riders will be disqualified."

Sam nodded. "Good deal," she said. "That'll keep people like you-know-who from winning the race, but ruining a horse."

"You needn't spare Linc Slocum's feelings on my

account," Mrs. Allen said with a sniff. "He doesn't know a thing about keeping his horses safe and healthy."

"That's because he still hasn't figured out that they aren't cars," Jen grumbled. "If my dad weren't his foreman, I don't know what would happen to Linc's horses."

"I'll tell you," Mrs. Allen said. "If that big beautiful Champ he rides should ever decide to run away from home, he can come to my house."

They all nodded and reached for more cookies, as if sealing a pact.

"Wait," Jen said, as her eyes returned to the rules. "Number three is a weird rule."

"It's my favorite," Mrs. Allen said.

Sam read rule three aloud. "'Competitor must be part of a co-ed team. . .'?"

"A male and a female," Mrs. Allen clarified, as if Sam weren't very bright.

"I know what it means!" she said, exasperated. "But—"

"Keep reading, Sam," Jen said as she skimmed ahead.

"'Together, each team rides the course side by side'!"

"The entire course?" Jen asked. "You couldn't divide it up so that each rider had, say, 3.4 miles—"

"No, Jennifer. Side by side. But you don't have to hold hands."

"Good thing," Jen said. "If you were riding with someone stubborn as a rock, like Jake Ely, and you fell while you were winning . . ." Jen rolled her eyes.

"You might get your arm dislocated from your shoulder socket," Sam said.

Although she laughed, Sam pictured herself galloping beside Jake. They would absolutely win, if he rode Witch and she rode the Phantom. She could see it as if it were a movie. Black legs would stretch to keep up with white. Milky tail would stream just ahead of midnight-black tail as they sped across the range, leaving all the other riders so far behind, their shouts of dismay would fade into silence.

But the whole idea was impossible. No one could know, ever, that she'd ridden the Phantom.

"That particular rule is what will keep my race from becoming a free-for-all," Mrs. Allen said. "A man and woman, or"—she paused and smiled meaningfully—"girl and boy, will have to travel at the speed of the weaker partner. The two who are most evenly matched will win."

"It's a great idea," Sam admitted, as her hopes deflated.

There was no way she and Jake would ride together. Even without the Phantom. Jake's riding ability was ten times better than hers. And Jake, as the youngest of six brothers, longed for a truck all his own. The prize money would put him lots closer to buying one, so he couldn't make a decision based on friendship. He'd be foolish to take her as his partner.

Sam sighed. Of course she could still enter. There were other boys she could ride with, right? She crossed her arms and stared at the piece of paper as if the name she sought would bob to the surface in bold print.

Apparently Jen hadn't veered off on the partner tangent the way Sam had, because she was still studying the sheet.

"And it's a benefit for the sanctuary," Jen read.

"To tell you the truth, girls, I made a serious error, starting the sanctuary in such a hurry. Oh, not in adopting those horses," she said, smiling. "But I wasn't very organized about it. I pretty much let my heart rule my head, and now I'm trying to catch up. You know the indoor arena I was building?"

"Oh yeah, that's going to be so cool. You can . . ." Sam faltered. "Was?"

"I heard that you lost it in the earthquake," Jen said sympathetically. "Clara at the diner told my dad," she added to Sam. "Five point one on the Richter scale is no little jiggle. It could have smashed everything around here into toothpicks."

"Thanks for the scientific analysis, dear," Mrs. Allen said.

She didn't sound sarcastic, so Sam had to ask the question she'd been asking neighbors since the earthquake. "Mrs. Allen, did your dogs know the earthquake was coming?"

Every horse on River Bend had acted strange before the earthquake. Popcorn and Ace and Sweetheart had been the most unsettled, except for Tinkerbell, the sweet, draft-cross mustang she'd been lucky enough to rescue from a slaughterhouse.

"No, they didn't," Mrs. Allen answered. "I heard most everyone's animals acted odd the week before." Mrs. Allen frowned. "I even asked Dr. Scott about it, and do you know what that young man had the nerve to say?"

Sam and Jen shook their heads in unison.

"He said that driving around with me had . . . oh, how did he put it? It was not complimentary." Mrs. Allen's index finger tapped her temple. "Oh, yes. He said riding with me had 'knocked their early warning systems out of whack'!"

Sam couldn't help giggling, even when Mrs. Allen gave her a quelling look.

"But the point is," Mrs. Allen raised her voice, "the arena wasn't insured."

Sam bit her lower lip. A month ago, she would have ignored this talk of insurance. It had been no big deal, simply something adults complained about, until the earthquake. Now, she understood. Gram and Dad had congratulated each other and thanked heaven they'd kept up the insurance payments on River Bend, even during the hard times. Because now, the insurance company was paying to rebuild the barn.

Sam watched as Mrs. Allen pretended to be very

busy brushing cookie crumbs from her sweater.

Everyone thought old Mrs. Allen was rich, but was she? Sam's mind circled back to the question Mrs. Allen had ignored before.

"Will the prize money be very much?" Sam blurted.

"Very smooth, Sam," Jen said, grimacing.

Sam felt a hot blush cover her face.

"I need enough to keep construction going until my next check from the gallery in New York," Mrs. Allen explained, not looking nearly as embarrassed as Sam felt.

Mrs. Allen still hadn't spelled out how much prize money they'd be racing for, but Sam gave up. It would be rude to keep pressing her.

"I think everyone in the county will want to do it," Jen said. "I'm already wondering who I'll get to ride with me."

"Me too," Sam admitted, and for an instant her eyes met Jen's.

She looked away. She hated the feeling that flashed between them.

She and Jen were best friends, not competitors. They couldn't be. Jen was a much better rider. She didn't fear going too fast, or jumping, or falling. Once Jen mounted a horse, she belonged there.

The Super Bowl of Horsemanship. Sam imagined a booming voice reading tall golden letters. If she rode in it, no one would think she was afraid. If she won, everyone would forget her accident. She might forget, too.

Mrs. Allen stood and swooped the folder up from the table.

"I'll drop a copy at the Darton *Review Journal*," she said, walking toward the door. "Who knows? They might want to do a newspaper story on it."

The girls followed her outside, but they stopped when they saw a black horse tethered next to Silly.

It was Witch, but Jake was nowhere in sight.

"Hey, Witchy," Sam said.

The black mare flattened her ears and glared in a way that indicated she didn't appreciate the nickname.

She'll eat you alive, Jake had warned her once, so Sam kept her hands to herself and stared at Witch's bridle.

Witch wore a mushroom-brown split-ear headstall. Faint feathers were etched on the leather. Sam recognized it at once. She'd given it to Jake on his sixteenth birthday, months ago, and paid for it with her own money. That was the last time Dad had allowed her to spend more than a few dollars.

That fact and the sudden creak of Mrs. Allen's truck door made Sam think of something.

"Mrs. Allen?" she called after her. "I don't mean to be rude, but how much is the entry fee?"

"Uh-oh," Jen said. She began shaking her head, amazed she'd forgotten to ask such an obvious question.

"Oh, did I forget to write that in there?" Mrs.

Allen tsked her tongue. "Well, my goodness, I guess I'll have to add one more teeny line at the bottom of my flyer." Mrs. Allen watched the girls carefully as she announced, "It will be one hundred dollars per team."

Sam was too surprised to gasp. She heard Jen moan, but neither of them could think of what to say.

Sam and Jen stared after the tangerine-colored truck as it bumped over the bridge, then hit the gravel and fishtailed like a bucking bronc.

"That's a lot of money," Jen said, finally.

"Yes it is," Sam said, but determination was gathering in her.

If she won this race, she'd earn something more important than money. Sam braced both hands against the hitching rail. She gripped it so hard, her nails bit into the wood. If she won, she'd show Dad she was a good rider, one he didn't need to watch over every minute.

"It's a whole lot," Sam admitted. "But that's not going to stop me."